THE DINING DETECTIVE

THE DINING DETECTIVE
James Vasey

ISBN: 9798296058836

Cover design: Mike Brough at Fresh Creative

Interior design: Diane Kane

Retail Price:
U.K:12.99£
U.S. $14.99

THE DINING DETECTIVE
Introducing Inspector Vittorio Conti
by James Vasey

Originally written as an outline for
a new food detective series set in Italy

DISCLAIMER

This story and all the characters featured in it are entirely fictional.

The foods, wines, and locations all exist and I have personally experienced most, but not all of them. The research has been arduous, but I hope it has allowed me to describe their main characteristics accurately.

Any medical or dietary benefits attached to any of the foods in this story are purely anecdotal and cannot necessarily be confirmed by scientific research. The author is not qualified to offer medical or dietary advice, and anyone should consult an expert before relying upon claims made by the producers of any foods claiming such benefits.

In memory of my much-loved and admired late brother, Eddie, who tolerated no fools, fakes or lawbreakers and could smell a genuine Taylors pie from fifty yards.

Table of Contents

TARGETS OF FOOD FRAUDSTERS

Sassicaia: "It strikes me that real, true haute couture lifts clothing to a higher plane through finesse." ~*Jancis Robinson OBE, ComMA, MW is a British wine critic, journalist, and wine writer*

Olive Oil: "If my cuisine were to be defined by just one taste, it would be that of subtle, aromatic, extra-virgin olive oil." ~*Alain Ducasse – three Michelin star chef at Le Louis XV-Alain Ducasse à l'Hôtel de Paris, Monaco.*

Honey: "Life is the flower for which love is the honey." ~*Victor Hugo - French Romantic author, poet, essayist, playwright, journalist, human rights activist and politician.*

Parmigiano: "Age is something that doesn't matter unless you are a cheese." ~*Luis Buñuel - Spanish and Mexican filmmaker who worked in France, Mexico, and Spain.*

Black Truffles: "Truffle is the food for kings, gods, and pigs." ~*Antonio Carluccio, Italian chef and restaurateur.*

Franciacorta: "It's a process that's even more stringent than Champagne, and as a result, the quality of many Franciacorta wines far exceeds that of even the most famous Champagnes." ~*Kris Fordham - writing in Condé Nast Traveler*

Barolo: "King of Wines and the Wine of Kings, Barolo is a wine worth devoting yourself to." ~*Battista Rinaldi - winemaker from the vineyards of Marchese Falletti di Barolo.*

Prosciutto di Parma: "Parma has an excellent microclimate for curing. Prosciutto specialists use a thin, pointed horse bone needle to assess the maturation stage of the ham." ~*Various unattributed Internet sources.*

Venetian Sopressa: "Sopressa Veneta got its name from the practice of pressing the salami between planks of wood, resulting in a straight, flattened shape." ~*Wikipedia*

INTERPOL: "The International Criminal Police Organization—INTERPOL—a international organisation that facilitates worldwide police cooperation and crime control. It is the world's largest international police organisation. It is headquartered in Lyon, France, with seven regional bureaus worldwide, and a National Central Bureau in all 196 member states." *~Wikipedia*

EUROPOL: "Europol, officially the European Union Agency for Law Enforcement Cooperation, is the law enforcement agency of the European Union (EU). Established in 1998, it is based in The Hague, Netherlands, and serves as the central hub for coordinating criminal intelligence and supporting the EU member states in their efforts to combat various forms of serious organised crime, as well as terrorism." *~Wikipedia*

Forward

My journey on the appreciation of gastronomy and all that it means to us, began with taste, followed by a curiosity of origin, then how it is influenced by geography, the way that impacted on social history and finally to the connection to sustainability and global food security.

I learned how simple ingredients such as salt, cod and spices, built empires, shaped history, and continue to be reflected in menus all around the world today. Today, these ancient connections are being lost as we deploy technology to bypass geography and seasons and defy nature itself. A typical Christmas dinner in northern Europe might well start with salmon farmed in Chile, prawns in Thailand and the dill to garnish served with it from Ethiopia, and that's nearly twenty thousand air miles travelled before you get to the main course and pudding.

In our rush for convenience and economy we have removed ourselves from any direct connection to what we eat, where it was made and who made it but at least multinational food corporations are controlled by regulations backed up by law. In stretching out and complicating the supply chains, we have allowed criminals to easily infiltrate these. If the route down which we had already begun was not dangerous enough for both us and the planet, this system has now left what we ingest exposed to crooks with no scientific understanding, standards or scruples.

For me, the antidote is obvious. We need to reconnect with the origins of what we eat and accept the limitations of seasons and geography. English asparagus and Scottish strawberries taste better watching lawn tennis, your Bellini made with white peaches will taste better in Venice and please, please visit Sanremo to eat their red prawns.

Inspector Vittorio Conti cannot always be there with his fork and Beretta to protect you.

Chapter 1: New Beginnings

From the Juliet balcony of a fifteenth-century rented townhouse overlooking the Bierkade canal, the couple raised two frosted glasses of bubbling Franciacorta in a toast.

"Salute, my love! In one hundred and seventy-four days we'll be back in Italy and free as birds." Vittorio Conti had calculated this was the number of days until his fiftieth birthday. On that day he could retire, having served thirty years as a policeman, mainly in Italy, but in recent times based at Europol headquarters in The Hague.

Paola tilted her head to one side and raised her eyebrows questioningly. "Firstly, where on earth did you find Franciacorta in Holland? Secondly, why are we celebrating one hundred and seventy-four days? Why not a nice round, memorable number like one hundred?"

Vittorio placed his hand on top of his wife's, which was resting on the rail of the balcony. He twisted her wedding band around her finger.

"Simple. I was in one of those interminably boring meetings a few days ago, and it made me wonder when I would finally never have to go sit one of those again. Then I found a vineyard online that would ship six bottles of this excellent Franciacorta to Holland. And they arrived this morning – the one hundred and seventy-fourth day before my birthday. So, I put one in the fridge until you came home."

"So, will we be doing this every day until you're fifty?"

"Perhaps. But certainly, every day after that, my love."

The couple had been planning their escape for a long time. They already had a long list of places they were going to visit and old films they were going to watch again. They had planned the restaurants where they would eat after the cinema too. Vittorio would buy some equipment and fish for dinner rather than villains. Paola was going to spend some time dressing their apartment in Camogli, instead of the wealthy women of the world.

Vittorio knew that there was a stress-free and lucrative sideline to be had for him in offering security consultancy to private clients. Paola's respected position at Armani would allow her to negotiate a flexible, part-time role working mainly from home. The move to The Hague had served its purpose in boosting his pension, but they could not wait to be back in their beloved region of Liguria. Squeezed between the mountains and sea, it had everything they loved, not least family and old friends.

"It still seems like a long time to wait."

"Think of it as just six more fat pay cheques, then perhaps it won't sound long enough."

"Ah, ok. You're right as always, darling. That's not enough salary days. The idea that I won't have an expense account, International Soho House membership, and be able to fly business class any more is a bit depressing."

Conti shook his head at her private joke because he knew that these things didn't really matter to her.

"I suggest we make a list of things we want to do in Holland before our time here is up. We still haven't been to see those Vermeers."

"And you want to eat at that field-to-fork restaurant that just made it into the Michelin guide."

"Oh yes! I'd forgotten about that. And we've never been on that boat trip around the canals," she laughed, "With all the tourists taking photographs of our house."

He joined in the joke, "Yes. When the boat gets to this point," Vittorio indicated the canal down below, "you can look up and say, "I wonder who's lucky enough to live there?"

"Six months are going to pass in the blink of an eye."

Chapter 2: The Letter

A few days later, Paola stood staring expressionless at the letter from the envelope she had just torn open.

"Who's it from?"

She didn't answer straight away.

"Not another parking fine?" Vittorio suggested between sips of coffee.

Still, Paola did not reply or give away any emotion. Vittorio crossed the kitchen and looked over her shoulder. He could only see that the letter was on health department stationery.

Finally, she spoke but seemed distant. "They want me to go to talk to the doctor after the routine checks they did last week."

"They've probably found you've got high blood pressure because of that job of yours," he said, not sounding at all concerned.

"That's probably it," she replied with only a half smile. "Anyway, I need to dash to get my flight."

"There you go rushing about. The case for the

prosecution rests. The defendant is guilty as charged. But remember – today, escape is now only one hundred and seventy days away."

She kissed him quickly on the lips as she passed by, deftly wiping lipstick from him in one almost seamless motion, as she had done a million times before.

"Ciao," she called, waving her hand over her right shoulder but not looking back.

He stood for a moment watching her cashmere coat billowing out behind her as she strode – like the catwalk model she had once been – down the narrow Dutch street. The smell of her perfume lingered in her wake while he began to ponder what had just occurred. But then his phone rang, breaking that thought, and he too was soon rushing out the door as he talked to a senior colleague about a major ongoing case.

"You want me to get the Eurostar to London today? Okay. Fifteen minutes and I'm on my way."

Inspector Conti had been at Scotland Yard in London for three days when he received a message from his wife that read, "Canal trip tickets bought. Vermeer viewing reserved. Sequenza restaurant table booked. I had to play your Europol card to get that."

She also told him that she would be back from Milan on Friday, that the table was booked for 8 pm that night, and the canal trip was on Saturday morning. Vittorio briefly wondered why the urgency, but his thoughts quickly returned to the complex case he was working on.

Vittorio considered his wife to be the least Italian, Italian woman he had ever met. Perhaps that was the initial attraction, he wondered. She was always rational and pragmatic – never overly emotional or fiery. Although everyone agreed the former model was beautiful, Paola was self-effacing and never did anything that drew attention to herself which is why working for, and wearing, Armani suited her so well. The understated elegance of their classic styles and fabrics whispered style, while others shouted wealth. On first meeting her, most would guess her to be a northern European – from Scandinavia, or indeed the Netherlands, where they were now.

Her actions during the week after the arrival of the letter were typical of Paola. Of course, there were tears, but only in private. Later during the day that the letter had arrived she had carefully weighed up the best time and way to explain the outcome of the telephone call with the doctor. She had prepared the words she would use when she told him the news she'd received. She decided what she would wear and rehearsed the responses she knew she would have to have ready to answer his questions because, while she might be distinctly un-Italian in temperament, Vittorio was the opposite. She also knew that he loved her more than life itself.

It was in the presence of Vermeer's famous painting of The Girl with the Pearl Earring that she eventually spoke the words she'd been dreading. In the end it was Vittorio who provided the opening by commenting that, unlike in real life, the model's beauty had survived five hundred years and would almost certainly live forever.

Chapter 3: New Broom

The powerful farmers' unions and the Green Party only voted with us because I promised to get quick results on this issue. The police are useless. What we need is a kind of Italian James Bond, but one with a fork and a corkscrew, as well as a Beretta," the PM told a small group of his new ministers at a meeting in Rome within a week of their centre-right party being elected to power by the slimmest of majorities.

The government was faced with dealing with numerous counterfeit products that were undermining Italy's 50-billion-euro food and wine industry, causing fury within the farmers' union, and resulting in negative media attention. Added to their concerns were the loss of tax revenues and the damage to the reputation of the Italian brand from bogus Barolo, pseudo-Parmigiano, and not-so-virgin olive oil. The problem had been worsening for decades.

In some overseas markets, Italy's Department

of Agriculture estimated that almost half of the products sold as Italian had not originated there and were therefore fake. This was not just a matter of misrepresentation but also presented a serious threat to public health. The criminal gangs willing to rip off Italian brands had no qualms about whether these foods were safe. They invented the best-before dates to increase their profits and the dietary advice printed on labels was, in effect, meaningless.

Existing law enforcement seemed incapable of stemming the flow of counterfeit produce. When Italians began to die as a result of consuming fake products made by callous international criminals without safety checks, the government accepted it needed a more radical plan.

"Unlike my liberal predecessor, I don't care if blood must be spilt, so long as it's the crooks' and it's mixed with the fake olive oil and crap wine these bastards are passing off as Italian."

Vittorio Conti was the only candidate whose name had been put forward for the newly created role by the minister tasked with finding such a man. He had contacted his old friend, who had been the longest-reigning Mayor of Genoa, who had described Conti as the Inspector Brunetti of Barolo and The Montelbano of Mozzarella.

"This man is the fucking Poirot of pasta," he told the PM. He explained that he knew the family, and Conti's father had managed some of Italy's best hotels. Before becoming a detective, his son had grown up immersed in the country's food and wine culture. Conti could smell a fake Franciacorta as sure as he could spot a pickpocket or a dealer.

Two weeks earlier, Conti had been walking their dog along the seafront when he received a call from his former colleague and firm friend, Enzo Palmero, that would eventually alter the path of his life.

"Enzo, it was kind of him to think of me, but I'm just not looking for another job, especially not in today's police force. Paola put up with years of me coming home from work frustrated about all the lazy pen-pushers and furious about the endless bribery. I've promised her I'll never go back to that viper's nest. No matter what happens. All that greasing of palms, political infighting, insincerity, and backstabbing is just not for me anymore. And anyway, I need to be here with her during these difficult days."

"Exactly. But those are the reasons why this is perfect for you. You'll not be part of the official force. You'd be your own boss. An undercover agent hired directly by the government and accountable only to the new Prime Minister. You can work when you want and where you want, with no desk or office."

"But no doubt just chasing white-collar criminals armed with laptops, and fancy digital printers to produce their fake labels. Techy crooks driven only by greed!" Conti replied dismissively.

"Actually, that's not an accurate picture of today's average produce criminal. There's so much money involved in food fraud now; the perpetrators are often highly organised professional criminals who've moved over from drugs because the profits are bigger, and the risk of a prison sentence is lower. They might wear five-thousand-euro suits now, but underneath, they're still just greedy goons with guns." Enzo assured him. "I thought that, until Paola has recovered, you being based at home and choosing your own hours would suit the situation. At least go and listen to what they have to say, eat the free lunch, and then, afterwards, if you want, you can say no thanks. Otherwise, you'll make me look bad. I told the Mayor that I'd get you to at least listen to their offer."

As reluctant as he was to go, the last thing Conti wanted to do was embarrass his loyal friend. He knew that he must have gone out on a limb recommending him to the mayor for this role. After all, Conti wasn't the most popular figure in the law enforcement hierarchy. He could imagine the obscenities that would be shouted at police headquarters if they heard he might be back investigating crime. Conti had been honest and, despite that, he'd made it almost to the top of his profession at Europol. Many in the force envied but also despised that.

Conti's intransigence began to soften. "I confess that I've always wanted to eat at Al Moro. I've heard they've got the best Coratella lamb and artichokes to be had anywhere in Rome. I'm sure it's not as good as the one at Zefferino's in Genoa, of course, but I'd like to see for myself."

Enzo sounded relieved at his friend's apparent willingness to change his mind. "I also hear they have an extremely expensive Gaja, which I'd order to drink with your lamb. It will be on the PM's expense account."

"If indeed the most powerful man in Italy even gets a bill." Conti joked, with Enzo hearing a brief laugh that had been missing for a very long time.

"Second most powerful man," Enzo corrected him as he made the sign of the cross.

"Ok, Enzo. Set it up. But they should be warned. I'll fast for two days beforehand and then eat all five courses with the best wines on the list before I say no thanks.

Chapter 4: The Offer

Before the first course of lunch arrived, the new head of the right-wing government began his sales pitch, repeating what he had previously told his colleagues.

"I want someone who doesn't necessarily always play strictly by the rules so they must also work very discreetly," the PM said, touching the side of his nose with his forefinger. "I'll back you up against your lazy and ineffective former bosses, but I don't want this coming back to bite me in the media. You'll report directly to me, and I'll provide the help you need without the need for a paper trail. I just want results quickly, not more excuses."

The lunch was attended by the Prime Minister, his Ministers of Agriculture and Finance, plus a fourth individual who was neither named nor given a job title. Conti guessed him to be from the External Intelligence and Security Agency. The former policeman listened and nodded occasionally. He discovered that politicians hate silence. One had barely finished a sentence before another began their attempt to sound more knowledgeable, to try to impress their peers. It seemed as though they viewed silence as a vacuum that needed to be filled.

However, the less Conti said, the more they offered him – open-ended expenses, flexible working hours, a pension and an impressive job title, Government Special Investigator, although he would be allowed to use Inspector when carrying out his duties to help to remove obstacles that a civilian may face. He simply nodded without commitment and carried on eating the food and drinking the wine.

The unnamed man explained, "Several of these products have their origins in China but often pass through other European countries before arriving in Italy. Alternatively, they're merely transhipped through Italy to gain provenance, and then exported abroad as if they've been made here. Whenever law enforcement manages to intercept these fakes and lean on the small-time couriers, there's one name that is often whispered with an obvious fear of retribution. It could be a nickname or an organisation. We're not sure. The name is 'Tooz'. Although it was first recorded as 'Tooz' by the officer taking the statement, in a later case, it was written as '2Z.' It might be some kind of Triad gang, but to be honest, we don't know."

Finally, Conti was shown the list of fake produce that the PM viewed to be the priorities. As well as Italian products well known to be faked, such as wine, olive oil, and Parmigiano, he was shocked to see honey on the long list. Since the diagnosis of his wife's illness, Conti had been at home all day watching his wife's symptoms worsening. The doctors were doing all they could. They had told them it was a case of waiting to see if she responded to drug treatment.

Conti spent some of his time scouring internet forums discussing his wife's condition. Much of the information he found was anecdotal and unproven theories; some of it was contradictory misinformation. However, one of the remedies consistently claimed to be successful were foods high in natural antioxidants. Honey was the product that constantly appeared in blogs and research papers. There was consensus that acacia honey was particularly high in these natural qualities, with many claiming astonishing results.

The brand described as the 'Holy Grail of honey' was not available in local shops and had to be ordered online. It was said to originate from a small area in Lazio where the Madonna Lily was abundant. The tenuous religious connection was well exploited in its marketing, and it was consequently the most expensive available. At this point, Paola had been taking it every day for about a week with little change. If anything, her condition had actually worsened slightly.

After reading the list of fake products, Conti suddenly became very vocal. He asked, "This fake honey. How do they produce that?"

The unnamed man explained, "Huge honey farms in China where bees are fed cheap sugar syrup. The bees never so much as see a flower. The industrial sugars often contain all kinds of chemical contaminants and sometimes dangerous bacteria."

Suddenly, Conti got to his feet mid-course, wiped his mouth with his napkin before throwing it unceremoniously on the table. "Gentlemen, I'm sorry but I must leave. My wife is sick and alone. I need to get back to her. I'll be in touch about your offer. Thank you for lunch."

The politicians were shocked. They were not used to being treated with such disrespect. They had assumed their offer would be grasped with both hands and that they just needed to haggle about salary and expenses. They were not accustomed to having their proposals so casually dismissed, although Conti was oblivious to their displeasure. He now had much more important things on his mind.

Chapter 5: Grief

"And you want to include many of the furnishings? There are some very nice pieces here."

Conti sighed. "I know. But they hold far too many memories."

He was running his hand over the polished walnut veneer of a card table that Paola had bought at a Sunday antique market in Ospedaletti. After protesting at her impulsive purchase without considering how they would get it home, they drove the two hours back to Genoa with the roof down on the Alfa and the table legs sticking up. They arrived sunburnt and windblown but laughed about that journey almost every time they used the table.

"There are a few items I'll keep. I'll send you a list. Can you get someone to make an inventory and value them? What the new owners don't want to buy, they can send to auction."

Wondering if there might also be a sale to be had out of this meeting, the estate agent asked,

"May I ask where you are moving to?"

"Camogli. I inherited an apartment overlooking the sea from my parents."

"Camogli is wonderful, and you and your dog will have access to the beach. Then there is the amazing fish festival," the estate agent added, salivating at the very thought of it.

"Si." Conti was not in a conversational mood. It had been a sudden but difficult decision to sell the flat that he and Paola had lived in for so many years but he could no longer bear the feeling that she might be there on the sofa ready with a book when he came home at night, only to find it empty. Every painting, cushion, vase, and lamp held a memory, and it was all getting too much for him. He needed a fresh start.

Two weeks later, he was walking along the seafront at Camogli with The Duke, as they had christened him, the West Highland terrier Conti had bought for his wife when she became ill. It was not yet 7 am, but sleep was elusive, and he rose early these days. The sun was rising behind them, warming their backs on what was a fresh spring day. When they reached the small, impossibly cute harbour, The Duke sniffed the air. Fishermen were busy on the decks of their boats sorting the night's catch. The unmistakable smell of freshly caught seafood wafted across the quay and into the cafes. There, older, retired fishermen were enjoying a coffee or even their first glass of wine and talking about the big catches of days gone by.

Conti, on the one hand, was pleased with his decision. He had closed one door but reopened another, which held better memories. He had grown up here in gentler times. Camogli was a picture-perfect town. Not too small or too large, with a strong sense of community. It had all the things you would hope for of a town this size in this location. The beach was small, with more stones than sand, but it was south-facing and public. However, not every town of this size had a prestigious four-star hotel and spa such as the Hotel Cenobio dei Dogi.

His father had managed the hotel for the last twenty years of his career. It had also been Vittorio's workplace during the school holidays. This was where he had acquired much of his knowledge about the kind of luxury food and fine wine consumed by its guests that was only served at home on very special occasions.

The lifestyles of the hotel's guests were far removed from most of the population of Camogli. However, the hotel provided secure, reasonably well-paid jobs for a significant number of people. Butchers, bakers, cheese suppliers, and almost every other tradesman in the town sold produce to the hotel. It was the economic hub that had filled the gap as fishing declined as the main employer.

Everyone knew someone who worked there or who supplied it.

It was one of the few four-star establishments on the coast that had been able to retain valet parking. This service provided another three jobs for men eager to drive – albeit only briefly – the Ferraris, Porsches, Bentleys, and Aston Martins that made it to the hotel through the narrow streets. The Cenobio also has its own small private beach in a secluded cove and a large, heated swimming pool. Vittorio had been allowed to avail himself of the pool, provided he worked hard and did his homework without grumbling. Around this pool, he met many beautiful daughters of wealthy parents. Those encounters had honed his chatting-up skills to a level of sophistication he would never have achieved with local girls.

Conti knew where the rich spent their time. He learned where they had been before arriving at Camogli and where they were going next. He understood the seasons drove them in a cycle around the world. Summers in The Hamptons. Courchevel or Gstaad in the winter. Early spring in the Caribbean. Early summer or autumn to the Italian or French Riviera. Never in July or August when the much-despised 'tourists' and Italians overran places.

Occasionally, the tanned, handsome teenager enjoyed flirtations with these girls that then turned to something more. Midnight sex on a sunbed on the beach or even in their own beds with parents sleeping in the room next door. If his father had ever found out he was sleeping with guests, he dreaded to think what would have happened. Fortunately, these girls were like swallows, swooping in to feed before departing again to where the climate was better and the pickings were, quite literally, richer. When he first met Paola, apart from her beauty and elegance, her lack of self-awareness was the first thing that struck him. She had all the beauty and sophistication of those wealthy women without any of the false façade.

He was glad he had decided to move. His memories now included better things from his childhood. Paola had grown to love this place, and Conti felt that his departed wife would be happy if he could find peace again here.

But the dark thought that kept returning in the warm, sleepless nights was guilt at having been the one who had suggested taking the honey. Who knows, if he had not done so, she might still be alive today. The only way he could assuage this guilt was to channel it into anger at those responsible. He had never previously been a vengeful man. He had leant on the side of lenience where criminal punishment was concerned. But that had changed. Now, all he wanted was vengeance. He could not imagine these crooks as people with parents, partners, or even children. They were insects that needed to be stepped on.

He could remove the guilt from his head if he imagined what he would say and do to these honey-fakers when he found them. He had started going back to the gym to get fit and ready for the day he would encounter them. He was sure that day would come. His mobile phone began to ring, breaking into all these thoughts.

"Everything's in place? OK. I start tomorrow. Grazie."

Chapter 6: Acceptance

News of the appointment of the man who would become known amongst his former colleagues as The Dining Detective had not gone down well with Italy's new Commissioner of Police, Aldo Menzi. Instinctively, he didn't like the idea of any detective who did not need to cooperate with his former colleagues or take orders from him. Additionally, he had been told that Conti was already known to be a non-conformist and troublemaker.

The Genoan had a reputation for declining the free football, opera, and pop concert tickets his colleagues saw as the usual perks of the job. He even refused invitations to lunches, dinners, and smart parties hosted by those businesspeople whose legitimate dealings were often hard to define.

Vittorio had seen these so-called 'perks' as little more than blatant bribery from those he was sure would expect a return on their investment.

His former colleagues felt undermined by Conti's holier-than-thou attitude and bitterly resented him for it. Christening him The Dining Detective was intended to be a slur. In fact, it was ironically a more accurate description of what most of they themselves did instead of police work. They ate long lunches and talked policing, but did little of it.

Now that he was out of the force, his former superiors viewed Conti as a defector who might undermine their authority and highlight the force's inability to deal with the problem of fake products. Despite a mandate from Rome demanding full support, the office of the Capo della Polizia would do everything in its power to see that Conti received none. Every culinary crime solved by the usurper would, in effect, be a personal slight to Commissioner Menzi's competence, he believed.

However, thirty years of effective, honest policing had brought Conti some admirers inside and outside the force. Former colleague and old friend Enzo was one of the few policemen in Italy who didn't need to fear for his job and his pension by helping Conti. Even the Chief of Police kneeled before Enzo's brother, the Archbishop of Genoa. Social standing in public life demanded that your children be baptised, confirmed, and wed by the Archbishop in his Cathedral. His family connection to that priceless privilege made Enzo untouchable, even by the Chief of Police.

Enzo also knew that his family position, so close to the Church of Rome through his brother, meant that he too had to keep everything above board. It was therefore fortunate that Conti had been assigned as his mentor when Enzo had first became a detective. The older man warned about some of his colleagues' worst habits and steered Enzo on a straighter path. The two formed a strong bond, which would prove invaluable when Conti needed police help with his new role. When he heard that Conti had accepted the job, Enzo placed another phone call.

"Elena, it's Enzo." There was a silent pause before he continued, "Vittorio Conti's friend and former colleague."

"Ah, the nice Enzo. I'm sorry, but there's another fucking Enzo who keeps ringing me, who's an asshole I definitely don't want to speak to. And, anyway, policemen don't normally call me on my personal number."

"You gave me your mobile number at Paola's funeral in case we needed to talk off the record," Enzo explained.

Elena asked cautiously, "How's our boy doing? That was such a shock. It seemed inappropriate for me to call him directly to ask how he was. It felt uncomfortable to be at the funeral of a woman I'd never met and stand there amongst all her grieving relatives and friends. It felt like people were looking at me as if to say, who the hell is she?"

"Vittorio appreciated your coming. He told me so. He said that it was a long way for you to drive."

Elena had heard from a colleague that Paola had effectively been poisoned by adulterated fake honey. The final painful irony was that it was a product Conti had bought for her. He thought its supposed natural antioxidants might help her recovery. In fact, it was contaminated with high doses of artificial sweeteners. The chemicals in these illicit ingredients further compromised an immune system that had already been affected by her medical treatment. This ultimately led to organ damage and her eventual death. This, the saddest part of the tale, is what has been eating him up inside. But maybe things might become a little easier for him, now he had a distraction.

Enzo brought Elena up to date, explaining Conti's new role and that he was likely to need help from them both but that he couldn't ask for it through official channels. He explained that his own boss had, unofficially, put the word around that no one in the force was to offer Conti any assistance. He told them that as he was no longer a bona fide officer of the law, they were not to so much as run a number plate check for him. Anyone caught even taking his phone calls risked

---

losing their job and pension.

Elena's role as a senior forensic scientist at Interpol in Lyon had brought her into contact with Vittorio Conti several years earlier. The attractive Romanian scientist, with her striking bleached white, bobbed hair, was an enigma in a predominantly male police force. She made no attempt whatsoever to fit in. Her spiky attitude and punk look meant that police officers instinctively didn't trust her, fellow scientists didn't respect her, and the conservative French in general disliked what they viewed to be her bad manners.

She had worked with Conti on several cases, meeting him in both Lyon and The Hague. Unlike many of his colleagues, he had neither judged her, asked her out on a date, nor tried to grope her. Conti was the only one who treated her with respect and kindness. Despite the fact, or maybe because, he showed no personal interest in her, she had flirted shamelessly with the handsome Italian detective. Only when she realised that her charms were invisible to him did a genuine friendship develop between them. Initially, this was based on mutual professional respect but began to evolve into something more profound. Or so she believed.

"Tell Vittorio if he needs anything at all to call me on this number 24/7. I'm going to save your number as 'Nice Enzo' so that I recognise you next time you call."

Chapter 7: The Motivation

Conti's grief was masked by intense fury. In thirty years as a detective, he had never been so determined to catch any group of criminals. He needed to face those who took Paola from him. To do this, he had to remain calm and strategic. Charging in recklessly could expose him and get him killed, which he wasn't afraid of if it meant he could take his enemies down with him.

The Duke also appeared to be missing Paola very badly and had been off his food and been constantly going back and forth to the bedroom where his mistress had spent most of her last few months. The hardened detective had grown to love the dog as much as his wife had. However, he could not look at him without thinking about her. On a really good day, that was a joy. Mostly, it was a constant reminder of his loss. This sadness drove him to bury himself in his work, believing that only finding those responsible would assuage his guilt.

In his new role, early enquiries involved assimilating information about all the known cases of fake food products, starting with honey. He quickly learned that those involved were usually not specialists in just one type of food and that there were several overlaps in the scams. Like drug dealers, they would supply any substance they could get rich quickly from. After establishing supply chains and bribing officials so they could handle fake olive oil, they realised they could use the same network for other counterfeit goods. In some cases, fraud was the sole purpose but, in others, it was a way of laundering money from other illegal activities.

His second discovery was that three main groups were behind most of the trade, although there were key intermediaries from other, less powerful gangs in nearby countries. Italy's home-grown Mafia had quickly cottoned on to the fact that this could be as lucrative as drugs with less risk of being caught and no punitive punishment even if they were. As home-grown criminals with extended families in Italy, they had no problem substituting inferior foreign food and wine to be sold, mostly for export, but drew the line at adding anything that would knowingly kill Italians. The other groups – the Russians and Chinese – both growing in sophistication, scale, and ruthlessness, had no such qualms about collateral casualties.

The honey that had hastened Paola's death had almost certainly originated in China. Conti quickly learned that huge industrialised honey farms were fast-tracking the normal, natural process of bees foraging on flower pollen. Instead, the hives were fed a cheap sugar solution, and the resulting honey was then adulterated with chemicals and even nanotechnology to improve its appearance and taste. The most sophisticated versions could even pass the lab tests sometimes carried out on sample batches at national borders.

So skilled had they become at manipulating flavours and masking chemical constituents, they could take cheap Turkish olive oil, dilute it with nut and vegetable oil, and pass it off as quality Italian extra-virgin. However, there were no checks on the potential damage these chemical cocktails could cause to people or, with the millions pouring in, no incentive for them to exercise caution. The scale of these arms-length operations and the profit margins involved were staggering. Olive oil was sold by the tanker load, and honey in container-sized batches. Someone somewhere was getting extremely rich and clearly didn't care if there were innocent deaths in the pursuit of wealth.

When Elena was told of his new role and why he had taken it, she took it upon herself to write an algorithm. She created an icon on her home laptop and called it ContiCom. She could enter any keywords or phrases into its database, and it would trawl Interpol's active and recent case files looking for matches. Artificial intelligence was used to read and draft a synopsis of the case in question, creating a database of names mentioned and locations. Whenever she activated the app, it would produce a list of any results it had found. It was an easy way of cross-referencing criminal activity with Conti's fraud targets. It would later prove to be invaluable.

Elena programmed the software to search not only for exact matches but similar names to those that she thought Conti would be investigating. It was this system that had uncovered a connection between a smuggling route from Bulgaria through Slovenia, fake Parmigiano cheese, and the name 'Tooz'. Any potential link to fake honey from China was, at best, a long shot, but the phony cheese was a real enough crime. Solving it would give Conti a quick win with his new boss.

With no better clues to follow, Conti packed a bag for him and The Duke before retrieving his father's old Alfa Romeo from its lock-up garage nearby. The car was two years older than the detective himself, his father having bought it to celebrate his new job as manager of one of Italy's most prestigious hotels. It had not been driven since Paola became ill. Previously, the couple had used it to make regular weekend excursions to their favourite destinations. They shared a love of food and fine wine, along with a passion for classic Italian movies, that filled the gap left in their lives by not being able to have children.

When Conti opened the glovebox looking for the sunglasses he kept there, he found the Faliero Sarti silk scarf Paola had used to keep her fine hair from getting tangled when the roof of the convertible was down. Unfolding it released traces of her perfume, and The Duke immediately barked with excitement. "I'm afraid not, my friend. It's only her ghost briefly saying hello."

Chapter 8: Prosciutto Di Parma

Conti had a quick success in finding and breaking up a gang that brought in factory-produced ham across the border from France and passed it off as genuine Prosciutto di Parma for three times the price in northern Italian markets. This gave the PM the instant PR result he so desperately wanted.

The pigs used to produce genuine Prosciutto di Parma are fed a rich diet of whey left over from making Parmigiana cheese. This deep connection to the area is the beginning of a quality process without equal. The salting, drying and ageing process is strictly controlled by law, and the ham can take three years to reach full maturity. A good-quality single Parma ham can therefore cost anywhere from three hundred to fifteen hundred euros. Rapidly cured ham from factory-farmed pigs, produced in bulk, can be sourced for as little as a quarter of the price from heavily subsidised French producers.

While he arranged for a truckload to be

stopped and searched as it exited the Mont Blanc Tunnel heading to Piedmont, Conti raided the warehouse he'd identified as the distribution point. Inside, he found a million euros' worth of fake Prosciutto di Parma, a sophisticated label printer, and cans containing some unidentified yellow liquid. It later transpired that the criminals were using this to paint the outer fat of the ham so that it appeared pale yellow and therefore as though it had matured for a long time

A sample of this liquid sent to Elena at Interpol later revealed it contained lead chromate, better known as chrome yellow. This highly toxic substance causes serious illness if enough is ingested and it had been banned from use in food production. This news allowed the seriousness of the charges against those involved to be increased from fraud to endangering public safety, which brought with it the possibility of a jail sentence.

"So, after all our hard work, none of that seized prosciutto as a reward for you, Duke. It will all be burned and the bones buried."

A disaster had only just been averted after one of the Carabinieri officers called to the factory tried to feed contaminated ham to The Duke. Knowing that the fake hams would all be destroyed, the policeman had cut a piece from one as a treat for the dog. The Duke had sniffed it suspiciously and turned away. At that moment,

Conti knew that there was something wrong. His anger at these criminals turned to fury at the thought they had nearly poisoned his only remaining connection to Paola. He asked himself, what kind of people knowingly paint poison onto food for profit, knowing it will be eaten by children and their parents?

For the press conference, instead of a long trip north to have his photograph taken with the actual confiscated products, the PM used a real Parma ham that was readily available in Rome. Neither of them wanted Conti's face or name publicised. No one in the press would know the difference in the ham, his advisors supposed.

Conti had only his dog to share this irony with. "Our boss is faking a fake with the real thing. What do you think about that, Duke?"

The PM's right-leaning Italian supporters disliked the French and the EU almost as much as the forgers of Italian products so this was a double win for the Prime Minister and his new government. The politician took full personal credit for this breakthrough, stating that his newly appointed undercover force had solved the crime. The local police were only brought in at the last minute to make the physical arrests.

Glowing with satisfaction at his appointment of Conti, he stated, "This is a warning to food fakers that we have a gastronome with a gun on their trail."

Most of the media present at the press conference were merely recording what was being said without paying much attention to the details. Food crime was a topical news story, but hardly very exciting in their world-weary eyes. They would all cover it, and the photo of the PM holding a lit match under the ham, as though the fake was to be burned, was a nice touch. That might even make the front pages.

However, if a major football team signed a key new player or an actress revealed too much cleavage at a film premiere – or better still, there was a gory Mafia murder – this story would be bumped to a few lines on the inner pages of the daily papers.

However, one journalist, Claudia Russo, spotted the potential headline in the 'gastronome with a gun' quote, including the tiny detail that the PM had referenced him or her in the singular. So, there was only one undercover agent solving these crimes, she concluded. Furthermore, the PM had made it clear that they were not part of the existing police teams struggling with this problem. He or she was a lone wolf.

As a foodie herself, the idea of a maverick food and wine expert roaming Italy packing a pistol appealed to her imagination. She was also certain it would appeal to the readers of her column. From the mail she received from them, she knew they were angry about the fast food and canned drinks that were becoming increasingly prevalent in Italy's major cities. It had been this trend that had sparked the Slow Food Movement, of which she was a member. Moreover, this was an ongoing story that could continue to develop and build a personal readership. She determined that she needed to find this solo gastronome with a gun and chart their progress in her column.

Conti was off to a dream start as far as his boss was concerned, but he was no closer to learning anything about the role of the Chinese in these crimes. However, Conti guessed that these early successes would earn him some latitude to pursue his own agenda when the opportunity arose.

Conti was also beginning to enjoy the freedom of his new role. All the travelling, product research, and meeting interesting food and wine producers were a distraction and therefore a tonic to temper his torment. He now realised that being at home all the time immersed him in too many memories and deepened his sadness. Everywhere he turned, he saw traces of Paola and their lives together. Being on the road was a welcome escape. He started actively looking for crimes taking place that were unfamiliar to him especially those involving businesses that were renowned for good cuisine or great wine he had yet to fully explore.

Conti's father's old car was in remarkable condition and fine for journeys of up to a couple of hours, but too slow and slightly uncomfortable for longer trips. However, the PM's generous expense account allowed him to travel first class on trains, and The Duke was happier with the extra space and the smoother ride to enjoy his long naps. Italy's extensive rail network criss-crosses the country, and journeys often afford wonderful scenery.

The only downside was that busy routes in and out of major tourist cities attracted opportunistic thieves. Unable to cease being a policeman, Conti had already spotted and restrained a pickpocket and a bag thief, handing them over to the authorities at the next station.

"Once a policeman, always a policeman," Conti had told bemused security staff at the station by way of explanation.

Chapter 9: Veneto Salami

It had only taken a few days for Conti and The Duke to solve their fourth case since taking on the role. It transpired that fake Salama da Sugo was being brought by ship from Tirana in Albania to Rimini in boxes marked 'Sujouk', the local sausage of Albania. Once out of the port and on Italian soil, it was relabelled and shipped onwards to America as genuine 'Produce of Ferrara' at six times the original price.

The fraud had been discovered when a truck carrying illegal immigrants out of Rimini port was stopped in a random police search. They found ten foreign men hiding behind forty boxes of Albanian sausage. The police, puzzled about why any Italian in their right mind would want to eat anything other than Italian sausage, became suspicious. Conti received a tip-off about this from the PM's office. The Albanian connection made the perpetrators easy to identify, but not so simple to bring to court. Within days of being charged, they had fled back to Tirana, but at least the local connections had been apprehended and the route had been closed for now.

As he enjoyed his morning coffee and brioche in Ferrara, he read the newspaper provided by the hotel. Conti was reminded by an article that the Venice Film Festival was just starting, and there was an outdoor cinema there screening classic Italian movies. He and his late wife had been fans of the post-war output of Cinecittà, Rome's state-run studios, although all of the films had been made before they were born.

They found the optimism in the stories, despite the bleak backdrop of the period, to be uplifting. An old movie followed by dinner at a nice restaurant had been an end-of-the-month ritual that had rarely been broken during their married lives. Since her death, Conti had yet to return to the habit.

He roughly calculated the value of the fake products he had uncovered since starting his new role as the Italian government's anti-food fraud Special Investigator. Already, tens of millions of euros of counterfeit food and wine had been removed from the market. His actions had helped genuine growers and manufacturers to sell their authentic produce at a fair price, on which the government would earn taxes. He had covered his salary many times over, he calculated. Moreover, the PM was delighted with his success and the media attention this had garnered for him. He and The Duke had earned a break from detective work, Conti decided.

Driving into Venice was an ordeal Conti just couldn't face, and anyway it was only ninety minutes by fast train from Ferrara. He arranged to leave the Alfa Romeo at the hotel where he'd been staying so he and The Duke could spend a couple of days exploring Venice by canal boat and on foot. The outdoor cinema was at Campo San Polo, where he guessed that The Duke would be welcome. Provided, that was, that he could refrain from barking at any cats that appeared on the screen. It took only a few minutes to arrange the bookings online as he finished breakfast, after which he packed a small bag and set off for the Stazione di Ferrara.

As the train slowed on its approach into Venice's Santa Lucia station, the city was bathed in the hazy sunshine it has become famous for – bright enough to admire its beauty but not enough to see its wrinkles. The Hotel Ca' Bonfadini overlooks the Cannaregio Canal and features frescoes and stuccoes by artists of the neoclassical period. Conti had heard it described as an inside-out wedding cake—unremarkable on the outside but spectacularly elaborate inside.

The outdoor screenings didn't start until nine

in the evening when Venice was totally dark so therefore the protocol was for filmgoers to enjoy dinner beforehand. Rather than revisit places with memories from previous trips, he chose a newly opened location that he had found online. Barco claimed to have its own fishing boat, known as a barca, out in the lagoon and landed fresh produce daily.

The young man running the front of house greeted Conti and The Duke, bending to try to pat the dog on the head but withdrawing his hand when the terrier quietly growled at him. As they passed a table on the way to their own, one diner was receiving a spectacular-looking, on-the-bone rib steak, and both Conti and The Duke caught the inviting smell of seared beef. Most of the guests appeared to be tourists including, he felt sure, several people like himself who were here for the festival. He could see film programmes on some tables. Several couples were requesting waiters to take photos of them, doubtlessly to record their visit to romantic Venice. This restaurant was too glitzy a place for locals, Conti concluded.

However, he too was in a holiday mood. Having already been adequately pensioned off from his roles as state detective and then Interpol investigator, his new, unexpected, and generous salary was building up in his current account. When his waiter recommended the special bistecca alla fiorentina at a hefty ninety-five euros, he decided to indulge himself.

"If I might suggest, signore, a glass of Sassicaia would be perfect with that. I have an excellent bottle of 2018 opened by another customer and can offer it to you by the glass."

Sassicaia is a costly, modern-style wine from French vines grown near Livorno on the Tuscan coast. It is aged in oak for several years and matures further in the bottle. A bottle of Sassicaia from the 1970s could be worth over two thousand euros and even more for especially good vintage years. Although the vineyards were less than two hours from Genoa, Conti had yet to visit them. He was aware of its reputation as a wine of distinction, but it was out of the price range of a policeman.

"And the price of a glass?"

Leaning closer, the waiter replied in a low whisper. "At lunch today, I sold two glasses out of one bottle for two hundred and fifty euros each to some Americans who said they would not pay the full seven hundred for the whole bottle. I can let you have a glass of what remains for fifty euros."

Recognising that this was a very competitive price for a glass of Sassicaia in a restaurant, Conti ordered it. Feeling only slightly guilty about his extravagant supper, he turned his thoughts to the evening ahead. A screening of The Bicycle Thieves, directed by his namesake, Vittorio De Sica, was one of the first post-war classics to come out of Rome. Conti had last seen it ten years ago with Paola and was looking forward to reacquainting himself with the plot.

The waiter arrived with the Sassicaia and proudly showed him the label. Removing the temporary stopper, he poured a small amount into a large glass. Conti swirled it around, noting the rich ruby colour, and sniffed it. It was intensely aromatic. Perfect for the steak, he decided.

Pouring the remainder of the glass, the waiter added unnecessarily, "You're a man of discerning taste". The intuitive detective thought he detected a note of sarcasm in the man's voice but dismissed the observation as irrelevant.

As the wine gurgled from the bottle into the glass, Conti was transported back to Camogli. He must have been fourteen when his father poured him his first glass of wine in the restaurant of the Hotel Cenobio dei Dogi. Reaching out to grab the stem of the glass he was desperate to taste, he was stopped short.

"Wait. First, you taste with your eyes. Read the label and note the details," his father had told him. Not quite blessed with a photographic memory, the boy was nevertheless good at remembering things.

"Examine the cork. Smell it. Does it remind you of anything?"

The teenager screwed his face up, his brain trying to work out the potential penalty of getting the answer wrong. By now, he knew how his father played these games. It did remind Vittorio of something, but he couldn't make the connection.

"Wintertime?" he offered hesitantly.

"OK. And what do we have to do in winter?"

The father could almost hear the cogs turning in his son's brain before he answered. "Keep warm."

"And we keep warm by...?"

"Chopping firewood! It smells of cut wood."

"Correct. Now take off your shoe and then a sock."

The boy looked at his father and then around the quiet restaurant to see if anyone was watching. However, worried that he was going mad, he did as his father requested.

"Now, smell your sock."

Vittorio tipped his head to one side in a questioning gesture but then wrinkled his nose, anticipating what he suspected would be an unpleasant experience.

"If a cork smells musty like a basket full of dirty washing then there's something wrong with the wine."

The teenager suddenly had a flashback.

"Musty, you mean like grandma's bedroom?"

His father half-smiled, tipping his head to one side.

"That is not a comparison you should share with anyone else. Certainly not Nonna, but it's true that people living in small spaces with little air circulating can smell musty. Now, the colour of the wine. Swirl it around the glass so that it paints the sides. On a scale where rose wine is zero and blood is ten, what number is this?"

"Number seven. Or, possibly five," he added quickly, giving himself some margin of error.

"So, you're saying six?" offered the older man, forcing him to offer a clear-cut answer.

The boy nodded in agreement.

Smiling at his son, he told him "Believe in your instincts. You were correct the first time. It's more of a seven."

Holding his own glass by the stem, his father swirled the wine and put the glass to his nose. "While we've been talking, the wine has had a chance to release all its complex aromas. Matching these with things you know will take many years, but you'll get there if you pay attention to all the smells that you encounter throughout life. Both pleasant and unpleasant. This will build a library of aromas for comparisons. Tell me which, if any, of these you can detect in this aroma. Coffee, nuts, cherries, pizza?"

"Nutella," the young Vittorio answered without thinking. His father laughed.

"Not bad. Nuts and chocolate. There you see.

Trust your instincts."

Vittorio smiled, happy to be getting something right and pleasing his father. "Can I try it now?" he asked enthusiastically.

"OK. But you don't drink wine like water. It is to savour, not to quench your thirst or hydrate your body. You need to pass it across the most sensitive receptors that you have – your lips and tongue. Pursing your lips and pushing your tongue forward until it almost touches your teeth, breathe in and suck from your throat."

Vittorio tried this but with too much enthusiasm, made a slurping sound and sprayed wine into the back of his throat, which was unprepared for its acidity. The inhalation caused him to cough and spray some of the wine back out. His father stood back to avoid being covered and smiled patiently.

"Practice. Just practice. All good things take time."

Light taps on Conti's shoe from The Duke, who was hiding under the table, brought him back to the present – his steak and wine. The dog was reminding his master that he was keen to taste some of the meat he was currently enjoying and, at the very least, chew on a morsel. Before he had finished his food or drink, the waiter returned with the bottle of Sassicaia, suggesting he might like another glass. It was fine, he thought, but not so great that he would buy another at that price. He did ask to see the bottle and the cork. The waiter held them closer but did not hand either over. Conti recognised 'Castagneto Carducci' as being the area of the DOC, and everything else looked as he would have expected. Without warning, he used his phone to snap a photograph of the waiter holding the bottle.

"Something to brag about to my wine friends," he said by way of explanation. Although he didn't look too pleased, the young man nodded in acceptance of this explanation. He asked for the remaining steak to be wrapped up for him to take away, paid the bill with his credit card, and left in time to walk to the piazza for the screening.

As he strolled over the Ponte del Parucheta, busy with film fans heading for the open-air cinema, something was troubling the detective about the restaurant he had recently left. Everything on the menu claimed to be the best Venice had to offer. It contained all the types of seafood the lagoon was famous for – canoce shrimp, folpetti baby octopus, and caparosoli clams. These are all delicacies foreign foodies would pay a premium for when visiting the city of masks. But these were also products that could be substituted, easily frozen, and brought from other places much more cheaply.

Tourists were fleeting customers who, by

definition, are unfamiliar with local produce. They rarely return to the same restaurant twice. They were the perfect victims for the type of scams that utilise the fake food he was being paid to stamp out. The only meat dish on the menu was the bistecca alla Fiorentina, the most expensive steak in all of Italy. Who but a connoisseur would know the difference between it and a good one from Argentina, Conti asked himself.

All these factors, combined with the conveniently open bottle of Sassicaia, which was a good red but not amazing, suggested to the detective that something about the whole operation smelled a little off. The final thing that made Conti suspect something was not genuine was the way The Duke had growled at the waiter. That dog was rarely unfriendly but could sniff a crook ten metres away. Even Venetians in their masks would not fool his finely tuned nose, he joked to himself.

While he was mulling over his suspicions, and as the film was about to begin, Conti found a single spare seat next to an attractive, expensively dressed lady about his own age.

"Do you like dogs?" Conti asked, pointing to The Duke who was wagging his tail vigorously.

"Si,.Sit." Realising what she had said, she laughed. "I mean you. Not the dog."

The pair both laughed at her joke, but then

watched the film in silence. Occasionally, the quiet snore of the terrier asleep on Conti's lap caused them to simultaneously look down and smile. Applause broke out when the end titles rolled, the lady beside him clapping vigorously.

She turned to him, smiling but with tears in her eyes, "That was amazing."

Conto returned her smile, "Yes, my wife and I have seen it many times. It's one of her favourites."

"Then why is she not with you tonight?"

Conti had become adept at explaining his circumstances without soliciting pity or getting into lengthy explanations.

"Your dog isn't a film lover? He slept all the way through."

"Fortunately, there were no cats in the story, because that can be a problem."

He began to decline gracefully, but then changed his mind and accepted her invitation for a drink at a pavement cafe on the side of the piazza. She ordered a Campari soda, and he a Negroni sbagliato.

She opened the conversation, "You're a northern Italian. Parma or Genoa?"

"I'm a proud Genovese."

"My football team also plays in red."

"Ah, so you are Torinese?"

She smiled. "I had a feeling that you weren't really a football fan. That was a test. I'm from

Milan. Both cities' teams play in red."

Conti laughed and then congratulated her on her interrogation technique. "Thirty years a policeman, and yet I have been tricked so easily."

By the time they had finished their drinks, Conti had learned that she ran a fashion PR business. He steered the conversation to rip-off designer wear.

Her face darkened, "It's costing the industry billions of euros a year, threatening jobs, including mine, and blatantly ripping off designers by flogging cheap fakes on the streets. It makes my blood boil. And the local police just ignore them."

Now sensing that the woman was likely to be receptive, the detective told her a little about his role but explained that he was not there on official business. He was supposed to be having a break from work and watching some old Italian movies. She confessed she was not really a fan of old films but saw the big open-air screen and thought it would be a pleasant way to spend an evening, so she took a seat.

"I was surprised how much I enjoyed a film made seventy years ago."

Conti replied, "A good story, well told, is timeless."

He told her that, although not actively looking for crime in Venice, he still felt it was hard to ignore something that suspicious. He described being offered the costly wine from a bottle that was already open, but with a plausible story to back it up.

"You're on holiday. Tourists in Italian cities have been taken advantage of for centuries. Does it matter that a few Americans got overcharged for a glass of wine? You said yourself that any evidence is all circumstantial. Maybe you should let this one go? And enjoy your break in this wonderful city."

Conti argued that these sorts of crimes were often just the tip of the iceberg. That behind them was usually a network with tentacles reaching out to other crimes and more serious criminals. He explained that, as with designer fashion rip-offs, it is not just a few street sellers making a few euros. There would be a global manufacturing and distribution network behind each fake, bribing officials and then laundering the proceeds.

"You make a good point."

Emboldened, he asked if she would be willing to visit the suspicious restaurant on her own the following lunchtime to check his suspicions, and that the meal would be courtesy of the government.

"You can have a nice lunch and get some of your taxes back at the same time."

"You're asking me to go undercover as a government agent? I hardly know you," she said, smiling mischievously.

"I suppose that is exactly what I'm proposing," Conti admitted.

"How exciting. How could a girl refuse?"

"By way of thanks, we'll also buy you dinner later to discover what you've learned." "When you say 'we,' do you mean you and The Duke, or the government?"

They both laughed about their minor conspiracy, swapped phone numbers and the details of the plan were talked through. They both noticed the fine-smelling food and happy satisfied customers at the cafe where they had been sitting for forty-five minutes. It was quickly agreed that they would meet back there the following evening at 7 pm.

"It's Isabella Fabbri, by the way."

"Inspector Conti. Sorry, Vittorio. Please call me Vittorio."

The following evening, Conti and The Duke had already been seated when Isabella arrived, looking excited and stylishly attractive, the detective noted.

"You won't believe it. The waiter offered me the exact wine by the glass with the very same story."

Conti did believe it. After asking her what she would like for an aperitivo, she launched into a description of the remainder of the meal.

"I started with the folpetti and black risotto, followed by bistecca alla Fiorentina with black Alba truffle, and finally, crema fritta alla Veneziana."

Conti whistled in amazement. "Wow, you really do go for it!"

"Listen, I paid a lot of tax last year. If this is my one chance to get some back, I'm making the most of it."

"Well, it's not your only chance because tonight's supper is also on the government. As an undercover source being debriefed, you're a legitimate expense. However, after that lunch, I doubt you'll be able to eat very much," he added, smiling.

"Don't you worry. If the government is paying again, I can eat again," she assured him, laughing.

Isabella took out the receipt from lunchtime and explained that it was handwritten. The waiter had told her that they were having issues with the credit card machine and asked if she could pay in cash. This made her wonder, so she had watched him tell the same story to several other diners. Some of them obviously did not have sufficient cash.

"But then the card machine magically reconnected to the wi-fi signal and was OK."

"A miracle," Conti observed cynically, making the sign of a cross over his chest with his right hand as though in a church.

Conti summed up what he believed was happening – that they had only one empty Sassicaia bottle that was half-filled as required with something quite acceptable, but not the genuine wine. And, if that is how they operated, he guessed that his bistecca alla Fiorentina was more likely from France or Argentina than Florence. Also, that his new friend's folpetti was probably frozen in Croatia and not caught fresh in Venice's lagoon, as the menu claimed. As for the truffle, probably from Albania and not Alba, he guessed.

Conti and his new informant spent the remainder of the evening savouring some wonderful light pasta with seafood, which the detective believed did actually come fresh from the lagoon. Isabella accepted Conti's offer for him and The Duke to walk her back to the hotel. Their route passed Stazione Marittima where a cruise ship was disgorging its mostly overweight American passengers.

Isabella suddenly pointed towards a man standing at the foot of the gangway. "Is that not the guy from that restaurant?"

Conti tried to find a familiar face among the passengers disembarking, but couldn't.

"The one in the suede jacket who looks as though he's waiting for someone coming off the ship."

As Conti spotted the man in question, he was stepping forward to greet two men in their twenties who had reached the end of the gangway. Neither looked like the other tourists, and each was wheeling a large black suitcase. None of the other passengers were carrying anything but handbags and cameras. The three men shook hands and then turned and walked off towards a side street, the case wheels rumbling over the joints in the stone paving. When they reached a junction, the two men passed the cases to the waiter. Without missing a step, the two men turned one way and waiter, now pushing two cases, continued straight ahead.

"Can you look after The Duke?" Conti suddenly asked Isabella, already handing her the leather lead.

The detective set off jogging towards the intersection, turning left to follow the two passengers. Without thinking, Isabella also headed towards the junction but took the direction the waiter had, with The Duke following willingly. The man pushing two heavy cases was moving much slower than his associates.

Conti caught up with the men as they boarded an almost empty shuttle ferry about to cross the lagoon towards the station. He managed to step on board just as it was pulling away from the pontoon. Once on the water, the two men had nowhere to go but equally, he had no access to backup.

Conti took a moment to assess the likely threat. Both men were wiry but fit and under thirty. They were dressed in cheap knock-off clothes that looked worn and dirty. Too poor to be able to afford a gun, he guessed, but they could easily have concealed a blade, he decided.

He had to make his move before the boat docked when they would be able to run in different directions. When he called "Stop police!" they turned towards him, clearly ready to fight it out. However, his shout had alerted the two crew. The skipper pushed the throttle to idle before looking around to check on nearby traffic on the canal and then allowed the boat to drift slowly. There were now three against two. Even so, to make sure they didn't try anything, Conti calmly lifted the lapel of his suit to reveal the Beretta strapped under his shoulder.

"Really?" he challenged.

The two men looked at each other as though acknowledging they had been caught. Then one of them suddenly dived over the side of the boat into the dark, murky water. The other simply raised his hands. The crew alerted the harbour police by radio and within two minutes, a speedboat with a flashing light was dragging the sodden man spluttering from the water. There was almost an hour of ID checking and form-filling before Conti could get away and message Isabella, apologising for the delay and asking where she was. She responded with a photo of The Duke sitting on her lap on a sofa he took to be at her hotel..

As he entered the hotel, The Duke barked a welcome.

"Digestivo at the bar to catch up?" she suggested.

Squirming up onto a bar stool, she smiled conspiratorially. "Well, it's been quite a day."

"I'm sorry for running off like that. But those two guys are almost certainly illegal immigrants, and if I'd lost them, they'd have been gone for good."

"So, you caught them?"

"For a moment, it looked like they were going to fight it out, but one realised the game was up. The other decided to take a swim in the canal. The river police got him."

"You need to take fewer risks now that you're The Duke's only carer."

It had never previously occurred to him that this was the case. Who would look after the dog if anything happened to him? Without children, he and Paola only ever had themselves to care for. With her gone, he realised he had become more reckless about his own safety. There was a time he would have called for backup before confronting two, almost certainly desperate, and potentially armed, young men.

Isabella broke his train of thought by asking if he had reported the restaurant, and he confirmed they would be getting a visit early in the morning.

"In that case, I'd better hand over the evidence I've collected."

Conti looked puzzled as Isabella started to scroll through her phone.

"This is the waiter pushing the two suitcases along the path. You can only see his back, but it's clearly him in that distinctive suede jacket. Last I saw, it was hanging on the coat stand inside the restaurant door."

"You followed him to the restaurant?" Conti asked, now looking alarmed. "You were only just warning me about taking risks."

"Of course we did. Didn't we, Duke?" she said, patting the dog affectionately. "But unlike you, Vittorio, I have no dependants."

"Isabella, you shouldn't have followed that guy. He could be dangerous."

"No. I had my guard dog with me."

She explained that the restaurant had been closed, but the lights were still on at the back. She could see a lone figure moving about.

"We pushed the door, and it was unlocked so I went in and called 'Hello. Is anyone there?' I walked towards the kitchen as he was coming out. He didn't look too pleased to see me, but then I think he recognised me from lunch."

Isabella said she had made an excuse about thinking she had left her umbrella under the table. The waiter went to have a look which gave her time to take a couple of photos. When the man returned, saying there was no sign of the umbrella, she apologised for taking up his time and left.

"That was very clever but reckless of you."

"Why so? I haven't had so much excitement in years. Anyway, I thought I was officially an undercover agent of the government. After all, they've been feeding me."

The photographs showed one of the large suitcases lying open on the food preparation table. It was full of what looked like black squash balls in clear polythene packs. At a rough count, Conti estimated there were over one hundred black truffles in just one case. The photo was not close up enough to be able to read the label, but there was a chance that they would still be there when his colleagues called in the morning.

Both tired after all the excitement, they said their goodnights and arranged to meet for coffee and a pastry at 11 am.

Isabella was surprised to find Conti sitting at the cafe with a travel case beside him and his jacket draped over its handle.

"You're leaving?" she asked, unable to hide her dismay.

"Sadly, yes, but I've got good news on our three villains. The youngest, whom I arrested on the boat, immediately told my colleagues the full story under questioning."

Conti explained that, as he suspected, they were illegal immigrants from Albania. They had paid for their passage by acting as couriers for the truffles as well as some other interesting items that his Venetian colleagues had found in the second case. A dishonest member of the cruise ship's catering crew had allowed them on board in Croatia where, dressed in high-vis jackets, they had carried boxes of truffles on board as part of food restocking. The men had then been hidden in the kitchen to avoid having to get off the boat before it departed the port. Once they had handed over their contraband to the waiter, they were free to disappear into Europe.

"Is all this worth it for a case of truffles?" Isabella questioned.

Conti smiled, "Well, that's where today's news gets more interesting."

When the Venice officers had visited the restaurant that morning, they found nearly a thousand salamis in the cold storeroom. They were labelled as a Premium Veneto product, made to a strict recipe from free-range pork cured with pink sea salt from the lagoon. Each one would have been worth fifty euros if it was genuine, he had been told. After calling in government food experts, they also found counterfeit cheese, wine, and olive oil. Added to the twenty-five thousand euros worth of truffles the Albanians had brought in, this was quite a haul.

What's more, the scam had clearly been going on for some time. Cruise ships were back and forth across the Adriatic three times each week. Immigration officials look for illegals crossing on ferries whereas cruise passengers are usually just day trippers and so pass under their radar. The products had arrived from Bulgaria, Albania, and Turkey, almost certainly via the same route. There were handwritten records in the kitchen showing that they were supplying several other restaurants in Venice. Those would also be raided by the Venice police that day.

"Even more alarming, the food inspectors were aware of a number of cases of food poisoning reported by tourists and are now checking those salamis, expecting to find that they were the source."

"These people risk public health and jail for what – to earn a few hundred euros?" Isabella asked.

"I fear that you understate both the motivation and the rewards."

Conti explained that the men who get caught live in poverty without the opportunity to lift themselves out of it. They see getting to Western Europe as the equivalent of winning the lottery. If some wealthy Europeans are served a different sausage than the one they paid for, so what, is their thinking.

"The reward for the real criminals – gangs running these operations – is huge."

"So you're telling me that we've solved a crime worth tens of thousands of euros, cracked a people smuggling ring and avoided a public health crisis," Isabella said, looking smug.

Conti nodded.

"Well, now I feel even less guilty about dining at the government's expense."

Conti told her that this accidental find was still a relatively small-scale operation compared to the cases he usually dealt with. Having already involved the Venice police, he could leave them to tie up all the loose ends.

"So that's it. Now you have shown me the ropes, you're leaving me to fight fashion fraud on my own?"

"I'm afraid so. The Duke and I need to be back in Genoa for tomorrow."

After thanking Isabella for her company and assistance, Conti extended his hand to shake hers. She outstretched her arms, insisting on at least a kiss on each cheek. Without saying anything further, he turned and walked away, pulling his wheeled case with one hand and holding The Duke's lead in the other. There was no explanation, no promise to call, and no exchange of addresses. As they crossed the piazza, the dog's head kept turning back toward Isabella. Conti kept on walking without looking back as Isabella stared after him, apparently confused and disappointed that what seemed to be so full of promise had come to nothing.

With The Duke still straining on his lead to look backwards, Conti said, "Come now. You know we have to be back by tomorrow. It's Paola's birthday, and we must take flowers to the cemetery."

Chapter 10: Parmigiano

"Stop." Vittorio's father shouted, sounding furious.

The last of three large wheels of cheese was being lifted onto the wooden shelves in the cool store. Vittorio was doing the fetching and carrying, working during his school holidays to earn a little pocket money. Puzzled as to what he had done wrong now, he looked to his father only to see that it was not he who was being shouted at. The chef was standing, hands on hips, looking indignant and defiant.

"What's the problem, Father? It's just a cheese delivery."

Dressed in his immaculate dark suit and box tie, Signore Conti always looked out of place in a kitchen that was full of boiling pans and steam accompanied by the endless chopping of meat and vegetables.

"Vittorio. What do you smell?"

Sure that this was a trick question, the boy thought hard before answering. "Bolognese," he offered.

"Not in the pans. From the cheese."

"Nothing, Father."

"Exactly. The aroma of that cheese should be knocking you out. I should have been able to smell it when I walked into this storeroom. Where did this Parmigiano come from?"

Vittorio started to answer, "Off a truck."

But the old chef knew this question was being directed at him. "I found a new supplier. Same quality. Lower price."

The hotelier smiled, shaking his head.

"In my considerable experience, those two things never come as one package. What's the name of this supplier?"

"They're from Genoa. Very reliable."

With a look to make it clear he was not going to settle for being fobbed off, Signore Conti asked again, "And the name?"

"Errr...Parodi."

"Well, how appropriate," he scoffed, turning to his son.

"And from your English drama class, what is a parody, Vittorio?"

Frowning as he thought hard for the right answer, he ventured, "A copy of something?"

"Usually a mocking imitation of something," his father elaborated. "And also, your wife's family name, if I recall."

"Half of Genoa is called Parodi," the chef sneered.

"The same half that's also crooked, I suspect."

Realising he had been rumbled, the chef changed tack. "We're getting this for four-fifths of the price of Fieschi's cheese. It's my job to order the ingredients and get the best value I can."

Becoming angry, Vittorio's father who was the hotel's manager showed no signs of backing down.

"The menu I give to guests promises Parmigiano Reggiano Superiore. It also claims our chef has passed the Professional Advanced Diploma in Culinary Arts. If we can sacrifice truth to save money, we could also get a cheaper chef."

"If you think these Americans, British, and other foreigners know the difference, you're crazy. They're all Philistines who put tomato ketchup on their steak and grated cheese on the seafood risotto."

"It's my job to know the difference. That's what the guests pay for. They put their trust in me to deliver what I promise on the menu. If you want to escalate this discussion to the director, let's get him on the phone right now."

With these words ringing in his ears. the old chef turned and walked away, mumbling to himself.

"Vittorio. Go and stop that truck before it leaves, and tell the driver to come back and reload this cheese. Don't help him."

This instruction was a great relief to the young man who had envisioned carrying the twenty-kilo wheels back outside.

"Then run to Feishi's in Camogli and ask him for one wheel of Parmigiano Reggiano and tell him it's for me and it's an emergency. That will be enough to keep us going until they can restock our shelves. Carry the cheese back here as quickly as you can. Don't be tempted to roll it, or you'll be working all summer for free to pay for it."

"But Papa, Feischi's is a fifteen minute walk, and those things are heavy."

"I know how far it is, son, and how much those cheeses weigh. I carried them myself many times. But by the time you've returned with a real Parmigiano Reggiano under your nose, you'll know exactly what it smells like, and you'll never forget."

It was August and when Vittorio Conti arrived, Parma's Old Town was a slowly simmering caldron. Its high-walled, narrow streets and thick stone walls had been holding in the heat day and night for several weeks. Conti had left The Duke in the cool hotel room, with the air conditioning on and a large bowl of water.

He found the address on Via Padre Lino he had

been given without any trouble, but finding the office itself was another matter. There was no name plaque outside, only a handwritten label on a mailbox, but no similarly named doorbell. He waited until someone exited the locked main entrance, greeted them politely, and stepped into the open doorway behind them. With no lift, the four floors of marble stairs were a challenge in the stifling heat, even for Conti who liked to keep himself fit.

The building was primarily comprised of small offices. But there were also sounds of a TV and a crying baby emanating from under other doors, indicating that it also contained a few apartments. Again, there was no bell at the door linked to the mailbox, but his firm knocking eventually brought out a neighbour from the next apartment

A man wearing a sweat-stained vest and unkempt hair growled, "What's with all the banging? I'm trying to sleep in here?"

Conti smiled, "Excuse me. Is this office ever open?"

"About once every few weeks, someone arrives and empties the mailbox and takes the letters in there for half an hour and then leaves. But that's it. Otherwise, I've not heard a sound out of there until you turned up, knocking the door down."

"Do they always come on the same day?"

"Weekends, when all the other offices are

closed. But it's always someone different dressed like a motorcycle courier. They access via a key code they read from their phones. I've only noticed because it looks a bit suspicious and I've got young children."

The office was an extremely modest setting for an organisation with a title as grand as The International Parmigiano Reggiano Supply Corporation, or 'IPRSC' as it appeared on the handwritten mailbox label. The office could only have one or two rooms in view of the distance between the doors on each floor. This was hardly enough space for a warehouse of huge cheeses, even if it were practical for anyone to carry them up and down flights of stairs. The whole thing smelled strongly – but not of premium aged cheese, Conti decided.

Genuine Parmigiano Reggiano cheese is expensive because it has to be produced under tightly controlled conditions and then aged in a very particular way for at least two years. During the strictly regulated process, each cheese is embossed with a unique serial number along with the month and year of production. The huge round wheels are then soaked in a brine bath where they absorb salt to preserve them. This process gives the cheese its unique consistency. When ready, the almost half-metre wide cheeses are stored on wooden shelves in a temperature-controlled room, cleaned and turned by hand every week. It is a laborious business that required patience and care. This care is reflected in the high price.

This exacting process means that at any one time, five billion euros' worth of cheese is sitting on shelves in central Italy, waiting to be legally sold as Parmigiano. Bypassing the legitimate Parmigiano Reggiano Cheese Consortium's quality production process and failing to age it properly was a way to make a quick profit. However, the fake cheese does not naturally possess the same crystalline texture and pungent aroma that genuine Parmigiano Reggiano cheese is renowned for worldwide. In fake cheese, these characteristics are mimicked by using chemical additives with untested consequences for the long-term well-being of consumers.

Nevertheless, the latest figures to reach the government suggested that sales of counterfeit Parmigiano Reggiano had caught up with that of the genuine article. Two billion euros were being lost to counterfeiters of the protected regional product of Emilia- Romagna. Established nearly a century ago, the influential Consortium, which controlled all official produce, was making officials extremely uncomfortable in Rome.

The Consortium had even threatened to send most of its premium produce to America, where

James Vasey

there was always more demand than supply, potentially creating a serious Parmigiano shortage in Italy.

Something as serious as Parmigiano rationing could bring down an Italian government with only a slim majority so Conti's request to head to Emilia-Romagna to find a perpetrator of the pirated Parmigiano went down very well with the PM in Rome. It would get the powerful cheese Consortium and farmers' unions off his back.

It had been relatively easy to find a supplier advertising the product to American restaurants in an online catering trade magazine who, despite their official-sounding name, did not appear on the Consortium's official list of members. Their simple business proposition, however, was a brilliant one, Conti assessed.

Amongst all the other importers offering Italian Parmigiano in America, only this one provided a 'marketing package.' The advert featured a half-metre solid olive wood cheeseboard accompanied by two handcrafted Italian cheese knives designed to present the wheel of cheese. The entire thirty-six-kilo cheese was photographed in a rustic-looking crate surrounded by hay, clearly stamped 'Prodotto di Parma'. A second photograph showed it displayed at the entrance of a smart Italian restaurant on its polished hardwood board, along with two fine-looking specialist knives.

The thousand-dollar price tag was similar to that of the other Parmigiano wheels being advertised. Still, this one appeared to offer image-savvy restaurateurs so much more. Conti imagined that guests who had walked past this spectacle would pay an extra few dollars for their bowl of pasta with some of that fine cheese sprinkled on it.

The advert led to a website where Conti found an address in Parma itself. No money was requested with the order. Instead, the buyer's payment card would be charged only when they received tracking confirmation from a well-known international carrier advising that their order had departed Parma and was on route. A nice touch, which made it sound authentic, Conti thought. The entire proposition conveyed an air of credibility. After all, the residents of Parma would surely not need to fake their own cheese, the Americans would assume. Nor would anyone be crazy enough to create fakes under the very noses of the Italian makers of the real thing.

After his initial visit, the former policeman decided that staking out the office would be a colossal waste of time. Instead, he emailed one of his relatives living in the States. He asked them to order a wheel of cheese for delivery using Conti's credit card. Sure enough, two days later, the email from FedEx stated the wheel had been shipped and provided a tracking code. As Conti had guessed, this code also provided a postal code for the point of departure in Parma.

The address turned out to be a drop-shipping, cold-store warehouse not far from the airport on the outskirts of the city. When Conti visited, it was full of all manner of food products from all over Emilia-Romagna and beyond, waiting to be dispatched worldwide. Using a convincing but bullshit story, he found out from a warehouse worker that the cheese in question was delivered in one big batch about once every month as existing stocks reached a predetermined low level. This news was not what the detective wanted to hear as it meant he could have weeks to wait.

If he could, he needed to see the truck delivering the wheels of cheese and try to trace it back to its origin. He had already learned that the plate on the delivery vehicle was always Slovenian. Conti knew that was not necessarily the place of production. The way these people covered their tracks, another transfer warehouse where trucks were changed mid-journey would not have surprised him. Hungary and Albania were well known for making adequate quality cheese cheaply. Conti felt that either could easily make a fake Parmigiano that would look like the real thing at first impression. Both countries were also infamous for cheap, unregulated labour, ignoring international conventions on brand protection, as well as EU regulations on food hygiene.

Conti needed to eat, drink, and think. While exercising The Duke, he stumbled upon Osteria Bini, one of the restaurants that had been recommended by the hotel receptionist. It was only a short walk from the hotel, so he had his first dinner there. The inside was cool and welcoming. Conti took a table in a dark corner from where The Duke could see the whole room, as was his preference. From here, he could watch any other dogs and people entering and decide whether they merited a sniff, a growl, or ignoring.

The cold-store warehouse worker had told Conti that it was a 21-tonne, four-axle truck that made the cheese deliveries. Using the calculator on his phone, he reckoned that if it was full, there was potentially five hundred wheels in each delivery, worth half a million euros – the equivalent of a scam worth six million euros a year.

"Parmigiano?" was the question a beautiful young woman asked immediately after his pasta had arrived.

"Si, grazie. With all the fake Parmigiano we read about, how do you know your cheese is genuine?" Conti asked innocently.

The girl froze and gave him a look as if he had insulted her honour and that of her mother and grandmother all at the same time.

"How dare you walk in here, a stranger off the street, and question my Parmigiano?"

She went to grab his bowl of pasta as if to take it away. Conti held onto its sides, and their hands touched briefly. Even as the words had left his mouth, the Genoan realised this was a highly contentious question. Still, it was too late to retract what he had said.

"Excuse me. I didn't mean to question this cheese, which smells like nothing other than the real thing."

He explained that he was working for the government, trying to track fake Parmigiano, and was merely seeking any clues on how an expert such as herself would spot it. The fiery Parmense told him they had been buying their cheese from the same wholesaler for two generations. Furthermore, even if they had been sold a fake cheese, both she and her father would spot it as soon as it arrived.

"First, we trust our suppliers. Second, we trust our eyes, noses, and tongues. The colour, smell, and texture are so familiar to me. Selling anything less than real Parmigiano would be the end of my family's reputation and sixty years of work building up this restaurant. Unthinkable!" she concluded.

The creamy pennete with Parma ham and mushroom sauce with shaved truffle was something to savour, as was the smile of the woman who had brought it, thought a very satisfied Conti..

"Did you make this? It's delicious. Can I ask your name?"

"It's Emanuela. This is my father's restaurant," she said, gesturing around her.

"Emanuela. I've a favour to ask. I'll only be here for a couple of days. I'm staying at the Regina Hotel around the corner. The Duke and I..."

The woman laughed out loud at hearing the dog's name, showing perfect white teeth but with a wide gap in the front. This feature was both unusual and, in her case, attractive.

"You called him The Duke? How funny," she said, bending down to give him a scratch on the head.

"Si, he's in charge because he likes to be treated like royalty. The name seemed to suit him."

"What's the favour you want to ask?" she frowned and seemed suspicious.

Conti told her that he was an ignorant Genoan who wanted to taste the best of Parma's produce in the short time that he would be in the city.

"I don't know where to go, and The Duke doesn't like to walk too far in this heat. I could waste my days finding only tourist trattorias."

Pointing out that he had a generous expense account from his employer, he asked if she could source the best examples of local produce and prepare it for him to taste here each day.

"The choice of ingredients would be yours, and the government will pay."

He explained that he wished to educate his palate on the best Parma had to offer so he could better understand the cuisine and be sharper at spotting the fakes.

The woman was flattered by the trust this well-dressed, handsome older man seemed willing to place in her and their restaurant.

She accepted his challenge with a simple, "Si."

He could not help but notice her silky smooth skin, the healthy bounce of her lustrous hair, and the confident sway of her slim hips. If she was an advert for this restaurant's output, few men would need any more persuading that it was a good place to visit he imagined, smiling to himself.

Chapter 11: The Meet

To the Conti family's dismay, the young Vittorio had chosen the police force as a career. Initially working as a traffic patrol officer, he had a powerful motorbike and a smart uniform and had gained instant respect from his peers. To the young man, it seemed like the antithesis of the life of the long hours in servitude his father had endured. Bowing and pandering to rich guests in expensive hotels for little money and sparse tips held no appeal for Vittorio.

He and Paola had married young. Predictably, both families said it would not last. After all, he was a police officer, a career legendary for testing even the most robust relationship. She was a beautiful and successful model contracted to a designer label. They seemed to be on very different paths until the day these collided.

He had stopped her for a minor traffic violation in Genoa and, much to her disbelief, wrote her a ticket instead of asking for her phone number.

After handing it to her, Conti smiled but said nothing more. Although angry about the ticket, she had really mixed feelings about the encounter. On the one hand, here was a police officer doing his job properly instead of hitting on women. But she could not help but be slightly disappointed he had not done what all the others had and asked for her number. At least this one was honest, she told herself. He also looked incredibly handsome in his dark glasses, cavalry striped trousers, and shiny black leather knee boots.

That evening in the hotel where she was staying, Paola was having dinner. A distinguished looking man rose from his chair at a table where he appeared to be having dinner with his entire family. The man approached, looking serious but kindly.

"Signorina. In Camogli, we have a local bylaw that it is my duty to enforce."

Paola began to get defensive. Yet, at what she guessed was in excess of sixty years of age, the smartly dressed man with well-groomed silver hair and a subtle smell of quality aftershave looked like neither a police officer nor a threat.

"You see, beautiful and interesting people who are dining alone must be invited to join the company of those with friends and family to spare. It's a law going back to ancient times," the stranger continued, smiling broadly. He gestured to the table where his family was looking puzzled but relaxed, while he simultaneously signalled to a waiter to move her place setting. His family was used to the hotel's padrone leaving the table to greet a special guest, solve some minor crisis, or reprimand a member of staff for not doing their job.

Paola was feeling lonely and welcomed the company, so she was glad to join in this lively family gathering.

"Having already got a traffic ticket in nearby Genoa, I don't want to break any more laws today."

"Pah. The police today. They waste their time harassing visitors instead of catching real criminals. "

"Vittorio, move over and get another chair for the signorina."

Conti thought he recognised the beautiful stranger, and what he had just heard confirmed his worst fear. He had been in uniform when they had met earlier and, although he had removed his motorcycle helmet, he had kept his sunglasses on during their two-minute encounter. He knew he might as well come clean.

"This is awkward. Allow me to introduce myself – again. Officer Conti of the Polizia Stradale."

Those of Vittorio's family sitting closest overhead his confession. His brother-in-law jumped up, laughing, and announced loudly. "Did you hear that? Vittorio has had to make an arrest to get a beautiful girl to have dinner with him."

Paola could see the funny side of this amazing coincidence and joined in with the laughter while Vittorio looked embarrassed. His father noted that once they sat down and relaxed, the handsome pair hardly paused for breath or took their eyes off each other for the remainder of the long dinner. They appeared to be in a world of their own.

Whether happenstance or parental conspiracy, that day had been the beginning of a love affair that would last a lifetime.

Much later came the realisation that they could not have children, often another recipe for tension in a marriage. Yet, if anything, that sadness drove them even closer together. After a decade as a successful detective, there came the offer of a change of direction. Vittorio was given a position as an investigator with Europol based in The Hague where he then worked for twenty years. Conti was glad to get away from what he increasingly saw as a corrupt and toxic work culture in Genoa. However, it meant relocation to a strange city in a foreign country where they knew no one.

Both he and Paola had excellent command of English, the commonly used language at the office, although neither spoke Dutch. They moved, and she made the best of it, but Paola's weekly flights to her office in Milan and back became arduous. Even though she could work from home some days, she still needed to attend lots of meetings in Italy. Nevertheless, they had survived everything that had been thrown at them, and it had just made their relationship stronger. But they would both not survive what was to follow.

Since Paola's death, Conti had pursued food fraudsters in several parts of Italy in the hope of finding the people whose fake honey had poisoned his wife. He learned a great deal about the way these criminals operated. He discovered a standard formula for selecting products to copy. To be highly profitable, the products to be replicated had to be capable of being produced cheaply where regulation was lax. There also needed to be a lot of added value attributed to the place of origin of the genuine product. Finally, they must be able to meet demand for large volumes, even at their premium prices. Parmigiana was a good example. Hard cheese could be produced almost anywhere there were cows, and for very little. If you could create the illusion of the lengthy, complex process attached to the genuine Parmigiana name, the cheap cheese suddenly increased tenfold in value. What's more, there is great global demand as a high proportion of all the fridges in the Western world contain some parmesan cheese. Or at least some hard cheese that claims to be.

Despite his motivation and growing knowledge, he had only ever been able to reach the lower-level criminals in these networks. He had arrested several truck drivers, document forgers, and other intermediaries, but they were merely the foot soldiers in the war. Those higher up the command chain remained elusive. The thing that nearly all those arrested had in common was that they knew almost nothing about who they were working for. Communication and interaction with their bosses were almost always at arm's length. Even the enforcement of discipline in cases of pilfering, breaching security or, worst of all, talking to the police was carried out by local thugs hired anonymously over the phone or the internet. No one could point a finger at anyone more than one level above them.

Trying to refocus on the job at hand, Conti had concluded that these were clever fraudsters. The perpetrators kept themselves at arm's length from marketing, payments, and the physical supply chain of the fake products. The starting point could be anywhere in Italy or, more likely, over the border and further East into Europe. The electronic payments could end up anywhere after being bounced around to cover the trail. But where was the hand, or hands, into which the illicit money eventually poured? A restless night in the heat of Parma's Old Town gave the retired policeman plenty of time to mull over the mystery.

The Government's Special Investigator was beginning to imagine a central criminal figure controlling a distant hub with a small specialist team who researched and sourced fake products. Using a tried and tested formula, these products were shipped by a variety of rented transport methods along routes that made them hard to trace. The cost was so low that margins were high; it did not matter if a truck or container load was stopped providing there was no trail back to the hub.

By morning, the savvy inspector had experienced an epiphany. The Prime Minister himself had said that, for him, arresting foreigners was not necessarily the most important outcome. Indeed, if the perpetrators were overseas, which looked likely to be the case, there was probably little they could do to punish them anyway. If he could deliver a body blow that cost the crooks dearly and close this supply route, that would be an acceptable and quick result for both the Consortium and the PM. Conti felt differently. He wanted them to pay, like he had. New tactics were needed that the PM might not like.

Chapter 12: Wheels Of Fortune

A violent thunderstorm over Parma finally broke the heatwave. When the water subsided from the gutters, the temperature in the city returned to one where Conti could explore the sights on foot. He collected The Duke from the hotel, and together they set off to Osteria Bini to taste the produce for which the city was world-famous at They began with what Emanuela assured them was the finest prosciutto and Culatello di Zibello available anywhere in Parma.

The Duke demonstrated a preference for small pieces of the former, which were slipped under the table to him. Conti moved on to truffles with seared scallops but kept these for himself, not sharing them with his dining partner. Premium versions of local wines, including Malvasia di Parma and Lambrusco, accompanied the delicious food. By the time all the parts of his plan were in place, he had eaten his fill at Osteria Bini. Relieved to be outside, The Duke had left his damp calling card on every lamppost in the neighbourhood.

Just as he was about to pack and return to Genoa and await news of movement, he finally had a stroke of luck. He received a tip-off via text from his new informant at the warehouse that another truck full of cheese was already on route. He alerted the PM's office which called the local police. They, in turn, alerted the media, as the PM had requested.

Meanwhile, a former colleague at Interpol had called the American magazine and given them a stern warning about accepting any more adverts for protected European products without conducting reasonable checks on the suppliers. They told Interpol that the next advert had already been paid for and was scheduled to appear the following week. They could pull the ad, but they wanted to know what to do with the thousand dollars that had already been paid for it. The French Interpol detective who had shared with Conti a love of spaghetti Westerns had an idea he thought his former colleague would find amusing.

He sent instructions for a replacement advert that read, 'A warning to the cowboys counterfeiting European products and those in America handling it: There's a new Sheriff in town!' Visa, Mastercard, and Amex were also notified to freeze any payments in their systems pending an international investigation into the fraudsters.

When the Slovenian truck driver arrived at the warehouse on the outskirts of Parma, he was surprised to be greeted by four police cars and a TV news crew. Conti stayed in the background, away from the cameras. The officers opened the truck doors to reveal nearly five hundred look-alike Parmigiano Reggiano wheels stacked neatly on pallets. However, following interrogation, it seemed that the driver had been an unwitting accomplice. He claimed to have no idea of what he was just a small part of, and they had no evidence to the contrary.

The loss of this one load would cost the counterfeiters nearly half a million euros in ill-gotten gains and close this valuable supply route into the United States. Not to be left out, and as if to add his own admonishment, The Duke cocked his leg on the hapless driver's boot while the TV camera was recording. Within just weeks of receiving the complaints, the government had its news story, which would appease the Parmigianino Consortium, showing that the government was acting. The PM was delighted with Conti's fast work.

Just in case the truck returned directly to the source of the fake cheese or, even less likely, the crooks met up with the driver somewhere in Italy, Conti had surreptitiously placed a simple GPS tracker on the truck. When he was released, the driver called his line manager and explained what had happened. He was instructed to continue with his schedule, make the two pick-ups for the return journey, and leave Italy as soon as possible.

With Conti following, the now empty truck continued to another nearby address, as had been instructed. Here, he saw several identical heavy boxes being collected, all stacked on a single pallet, before heading north again in the direction of Milan. After the truck had left the second stop, Conti visited the address. There, he found a supplier of the specialist linen and muslin fabrics used in cheese production.

"Is it used for Parmigiano Reggiano?" the former policeman asked.

"Si, solo Parmigiano Reggiano." It was explained to him that only cheese of that price could afford to use linen of this quality.

"But this order was paid for by a company with an address in Tus, Iran. They can't make Parmigiano in Iran."

"What do I know about Iran?" the man said, shrugging his shoulders. "I only sell cheesecloth. I don't check to see if customers are making shirts out of it."

Conti could now see where Elena's database connection originated. Tus could sound enough like Tooz.

So, the fakers were even using the correct linen to get the authentic outer texture on the wheels, he concluded. This discovery could only mean that these packages of Parma linen were headed back to wherever the cheese was being made. The truck made another stop, presumably to collect another return load from a warehouse at Milan Airport. It then headed toward Venice where he had calculated the driver's tachograph would require him to stop and rest for several hours.

This delay would give Conti time to decide what to do before the truck could leave Venice and reach the border with Slovenia, where Italian police jurisdiction would come to an end. Milan officers were dispatched to the warehouse at the airport to discover the size of the load and its origin. Six crates, sitting on pallets that had originated in China, had earlier been loaded onto the nearly empty truck. They were told the manifest said the crates contained spare parts for farming equipment. Instinctively, Conti thought this sounded suspicious and was intrigued by the Chinese connection. He needed to know what was in those boxes.

It only took a brief telephone conversation between Conti and the police inspector in Parma for the truck to be stopped and searched again. If nothing else, they would prevent the linen from falling into the hands of the counterfeiters. They had evidence that this material was part of a crime, so they had plenty of justification to conduct another search. Once it crossed out of Italy, there was little they could do. The counterfeiters would simply find another warehouse and alternative route.

From the tracker, they could estimate approximately where the driver would have to stop to rest. Two cars from Venice, equipped with a warrant and two crowbars, were dispatched to the area. Monitoring the GPS tracker, Conti could see no evidence of the truck stopping for any length of time. He concluded that the driver must have received new orders from his dispatcher to keep going until he crossed the border before resting. The tracker charted the vehicle skirting Venice's western fringes, by then only an hour from the nearest border crossing.

In the evening rush-hour traffic, even the police cars struggled to catch up on the lead the truck had on them. Even when they got within sight of the truck, it wasn't easy to spot it amongst all the other foreign commercial vehicles heading north. With only twenty kilometres to spare, the police spotted the registration plate they were looking for, and their blue lights brought the truck to a halt at the side of the road.

Soon after, Conti received photos from an officer's phone. They showed that the crates had been broken open, revealing several large, semi-circular metal parts and threaded stainless steel rods with large wing nuts. These had all been carefully engineered in gleaming stainless steel. To the untrained eye, they could easily have been agricultural equipment and spares, as stated on the manifest.

"Looks like our run of luck has ended," the officer told Conti but he asked the officer to remove some of the items and video them from all angles.

"There's the answer," he said, smiling. Both men could now clearly see the words that read 'Parmigiano Reggiano' as a mirror image. There were more moulds to stamp the fake credentials into the cheese.

Something as blatantly fraudulent as this could have easily been sourced from somewhere in China.

Conti concluded that, with hundreds of metres of cheesecloth and what appeared to be in the region of fifty new moulds, it seemed they were gearing up to substantially increase production. He instructed the officers to leave the GPS tracker where it was and accompany the truck to the police station. Here, they would have all the cargo removed, the driver would be interviewed again, and his phone would be examined to determine who had called him. They were then to stamp the driver's passport as 'deported' and escort him and the truck to the border. Conti would wait to learn the numbers of the callers and see where the truck went from there.

Even though he had captured half a million euros worth of fake cheese and halted the expansion of a major fraud, at least for now, Conti was only a tiny step closer to the ringleaders. What was the significance of the Iranian and Chinese connections? He needed to know. He had planned to drive straight home after the interception at the warehouse, but events had dragged on for several hours. He also decided he had earned one last dinner in the wonderful city of Parma. When he entered the restaurant, Emanuela beamed in surprise. They hugged like long-lost friends as they each kissed on both cheeks while The Duke barked enthusiastically.

"We thought you'd gone back to Genoa?"

"The Duke and I have earned a night off, and I couldn't resist one last lesson in cooking from the best in Parma."

Chapter 13: Taggiasca Olive Oil

Olive oil was the product that the Italian food fakers had already started to produce decades earlier. In recent years, demand had risen dramatically while supply dropped due to problems with disease and climate. Consequently, the price had tripled in just eight years. With 350 million litres of the precious liquid exported from Italy around the world, it is no surprise that this was the first target for counterfeiters. Inferior oil could be bought cheaply from Greece, Tunisia, Portugal, Morocco, Syria, and Spain, without too many questions being asked as to where it was going.

Bulk tankers full of green gold crisscrossed the Mediterranean every day, heading who knows where. Olive oil can also be easily blended with other products, such as nut oil and even cheaper vegetable oil. Consumers rely entirely upon the printed paper label on the bottle to judge the quality of its contents and origin. It is just too easy to adulterate content, create fake packaging, and make a fortune. A single load could yield millions in illicit profits.

In the Conti household, the approach of the year's end meant a long weekend at their family's orto in the hills near Avegno. It had been two generations since any of the family had once lived in the now fallen-down stone rustico, but they retained a couple of hectares of sloping land surrounding it. The twenty or so olive trees on these steep terraces had kept the extended family in oil for as long as anyone could remember. Harvesting was a backbreaking but thankfully brief task, usually completed in two to three days, depending on how many family members could be cajoled or shamed into helping. Vittorio himself had tried every trick he could think of to get out of going but, as one of the youngest and fittest, had yet to succeed in being excused. Oil was just too essential, even overriding schoolwork and minor ailments.

In his grandma's day, olive oil represented survival. It was fuel, lighting, cooking, medicine, personal hygiene, lubrication, and food preservative. Today, it was more a mixture of tradition, prudent housekeeping, and pride in a product whose provenance was without question. Vittorio could remember asking why they drove carloads of heavy olives eight kilometres up winding mountain roads to an old watermill.

"There's a big new mill downhill in Avegno, five minutes away," he had pointed out.

"Pah! They'll suck the goodness out of my olives, the lira out of my pockets, and then give me back oil I wouldn't put in my car engine, let alone my stomach," his grandfather had told him.

When he had asked why, he told Vittorio that the new mill used heat and additives to extract more but inferior quality oil. That heat also costs money. He told him that the cold press at the old watermill "Put nothing in and took nothing out. It's as pure as nature intended and has kept me and your grandma going for nearly ninety years. My mother was one hundred and six when a fall on the stone stairs finally took her. Otherwise, I think she'd have made another decade."

Not satisfied with this anecdotal explanation, when Vittorio returned to school, he asked his science teacher if it was true. She said that his grandfather was correct, and that cold-filtered olive oil had been proven to contain more nutrients and antioxidants than modern methods. His grandfather had made it to ninety-five, only succumbing to a virus while in hospital for a minor fracture to be tended to. His wife was still living with the family and cooking most days, a testament to his grandparents' beliefs, he decided.

Enzo had brought Conti's attention to a

potential new fraud case almost on their doorstep. Sanremo was a fashionable Ligurian resort famous for its casino, annual music festival, and sweet red prawns caught from its harbour. The timing seemed opportune because Sanremo red prawns were beginning to be brought ashore around this time of year.

The town was also a little over an hour's drive from his home near Genoa, along roads with views to rival the more famous Amalfi Coast, but without the terrifying cliff-edge drops. Vittorio packed a bag for himself and The Duke, put the roof down on his father's old car, and set off early, westbound. He was happy that the sun was rising in the rear-view mirror and not blinding him as he navigated the sweeping corners of this often narrow two-lane road.

When a UK chef, Eva Bonetti, recently awarded her first Michelin star, had been approached to endorse a premium Italian olive oil, it was not a difficult decision. The offer was from an agent of the brand of cold-pressed Extra Virgin Taggiasca olive oil made by the Bruzzone family, which she already used. In fact, she had previously effectively endorsed it by featuring a bottle in her first cookbook, which was likely what had brought them to her door. She had discovered the excellent olive oil at a Slow Food event in London, bought a case, and had used it ever since. In her new role as its brand ambassador, she would earn a small percentage of UK sales but, more importantly, a free supply of olive oil for her kitchen. She would also have her name and picture on the label, raising her business profile.

What drew her to the product was its provenance and long family history in olive farming. It came from the lower slopes of the Maritime Alps, a coastal region of Italy overlooking the Mediterranean, not far from Sanremo. On a visit to see the olive groves above the town of Taggia, she was told that the higher altitude meant the trees stayed cooler in summer. However, their south-facing slopes still meant they received the full heat of the Mediterranean sun all day except, that was, when frequent mists drifted down from the Alps above, enveloping the trees in much-needed moisture before retracting again. It was a compelling story, she believed.

It was also true that this unique but challenging environment kept the olives smaller than varieties from lower and hotter climes. Still, it also endowed them with a more intense bittersweet flavour. Because the olives were of a smaller size, it took more of them to make a litre of oil. The steep, narrow terraces would not allow harvesting by machine, so everything had to be done by hand. All of this made Taggiasca olive oil more expensive. Nevertheless, the chef decided that even the hefty trade price of twenty-five euros per litre was worth paying for a product this good, with a story so compelling.

She had hosted her own TV cooking show, focusing on recipes from lesser-known regions of Italy. The success of the series drove her previously released cookbook up the sales chart. In this book, she had endorsed the oil brand, and several photos showed her liberally drizzling a clearly labelled bottle of it onto her dishes. Previously only available from specialist Italian delis, supermarkets were soon asked why they didn't stock it. A deal was struck, and within months, newly labelled bottles featuring a photograph of the now-famous young chef were appearing on supermarket shelves throughout the UK.

This phenomenal upsurge in both shelf presence and sales prompted better-known competitors to wonder how this previously unheard of producer could so quickly scale up production. The annual olive harvest had been over months ago, and a new crop would not be available until November at the earliest. Had the manufacturer been sitting on a lake of olive oil, expecting this dramatic turn of events, it would have caused some competitors to ask. The disgruntled neighbouring growers thought this highly unlikely. This complaint was the source of the accusation that had filtered through to Conti via Enzo.

Olive oil is the most commonly misdescribed or mis-sold Italian product in the world, with some estimates that as much as half of what is on the market outside of Italy is incorrectly labelled. Some of these products have tenuously legal but highly misleading branding. These hint at an Italian origin using graphics or flags and use words like Extra, Original, and Pure. At a glance at the shelf in a shop containing many other similar-looking bottles, it would be easy to be fooled. Many people are duped in this way every day.

Others are more blatant frauds containing oils sourced from other countries but labelled Italian Extra Virgin. Oil from countries such as Turkey, Greece, Morocco, Syria, and Spain is mislabelled as Italian. The ninety million Euros Italy receives in tax revenues from exported olive oil could be doubled if some of this fraud could be halted.

First things first, Conti had decided as he drove up to the Hotel Lolli Palace in Sanremo in plenty of time for lunch. This hotel had been his and Paola's favourite weekend getaway. The Belle Époque architecture of the room was as imposing as the views out over the Riviera. There was a large gilt mirror over the fireplace, which featured a prominent bullet hole. This damage was the legacy of long-gone Nazi occupiers. The owners said it was shot in frustration over the – deliberately – slow service provided by the locals, which they saw as a way of showing their disrespect for their captors. The hotel owners had left the bullet embedded there as an act of defiance.

He was greeted with a warm smile and open arms by Guido, a member of the extended family who ran the old hotel. "Signore Conti and the young Duke. Just a puppy, the last time we saw you. And will Paola be joining you later?"

The pained expression on Vittorio Conti's face gave Guido his answer, and he made a cross with his right hand. "Isabella will be heartbroken. She was saying how much better she looked on your last visit."

"Things took a sudden and unexpected turn for the worse, and it was over quite quickly," Conti told him.

"God works in mysterious ways." There was a pause while Guido checked the hotel's register. "Although it's still out of season, I'm afraid your usual room is occupied."

Conti waved his hand dismissively and told him that he would prefer a different room anyway. "Too many memories, both for me and The Duke."

Guido handed him the keys to the second-best room in the hotel, with a balcony and wonderful views over the sea.

"And a table for lunch?"

"Of course, Guido."

A small plate of fritto misto followed by spaghetti with Sanremo red prawns washed down with a glass or two of Pigato from Riviera Ligure di Ponente. There were few things that The Duke liked better than prawn heads, and so both were well satisfied when they left the dining room. The olive oil offered to him at the hotel to drizzle over his pasta was local Extra Virgin Taggiasca, but not the brand he had come to investigate.

He asked the waiter if he had heard of the manufacturer being under suspicion, but without suggesting there might be any problem.

"Si Signore. Multo famoso e di successo," answered the local, fluttering one hand and sucking in air in the way Italians sometimes do to signify serious wealth. The waiter explained that the old family business had plodded along for generations, initially making a decent living but seemingly declining year by year as bigger, more modern producers undercut them.

That is, until the father had died a few years earlier leaving the business to be run by his youngest son and his American fiancée. Since then, he said that there had been what appeared to be an almost miraculous turnaround in fortunes.

Both Conti and the dog needed to stretch their legs, so they set off, passing the famous casino and heading into the pedestrianised shopping street lined with fantastic old buildings that housed designer clothing stores. When the shopping street ended after Sanremo's famous Ariston Theatre, they turned toward the seafront. As they passed Restaurant Flipper, Conti smiled for two reasons – the lovable dolphin character from childhood TV shows was a fond memory, as was the last lunch he had eaten there with his late wife. On an impulse, he called in and reserved a table for dinner the following night and then they continued their stroll until they reached the police station, which was their ultimate destination.

His old friend Enzo was now based here in Sanremo. Rather than go in and possibly be recognised, he messaged his private mobile number. Enzo emerged from the front door a few minutes later. Conti whistled from across the street, where he had taken a table at a street cafe.

Enzo told Conti that he had been doing some checking and asking around. He had learned that the two sons of the old olive farmer had lived in America with their mother after their parents divorced when the boys were in their early teens. There, the boys had both gone on to study at university. He had heard vague rumours that both the boys had been a massive disappointment to their father. They seldom called him, never visited, and showed no interest whatsoever in the farm. The younger one studied art and the older one studied business but both had only just scraped a degree.

The son who had eventually returned to take over the farm had not come to the attention of local police. His fiancée, on the other hand, had become quite renowned as the scourge of local restaurants. She had gained a reputation as being arrogant, unreasonable, and rude to staff.

"Flipper and its sister restaurant at the port have told her husband that his wife is not welcome there," Enzo told him with a certain glee.

"No one is sure why the son had a sudden change of heart about farming, but everyone's guess is the surge in the price of olive oil. One more thing. I've had a reporter asking questions about you. Someone called Claudia Russo called me yesterday. She said a police source in Rome had informed her that the head of the PM's new force investigating food fraud was a detective from Genoa. One of our helpful former colleagues there gave her my name."

Enzo told his friend that he had tried to put her off the trail, saying that he had not seen Conti since his wife's funeral. "But that I'd heard you were travelling and taking time to grieve. You were certainly no longer in the police force."

"All of which is true. Thank you, Enzo. What do you suppose she wants?"

Enzo raised both hands with upturned palms

to indicate that he had no idea.

The farm offered olive oil tastings to the public and operated a farm shop. Conti was able to book a tasting online for the following day via the company website. He and The Duke enjoyed the scenic drive up to Seborga from the coast. The sun was out, and he could smell the flowers that lined the road on either side in an array of colours. Occasionally, the road twisted back on itself and then offered stunning views out over the glistening Mediterranean. The olive oil of Seborga and the surrounding area is thought by many to be the best in the world because of its unique geographic position midway between the Mediterranean Sea and the Maritime Alps. The olive trees on its elevated, south facing slopes are bathed in sunshine but also alternately moistened by warm sea and cool mountain breezes.

Beyond the ancient village of Seborga, the road became narrower and more challenging. It was a single-track road with only passing places, meaning Conti had to slow his driving pace. As he approached one bend, a small tanker appeared, forcing him to stop and reverse to the previous passing place. When he finally arrived at the olive mill and farmhouse where the tasting was taking place, a minibus had parked up and its last passenger was disembarking.

The tour involved just a hundred metre stroll

to where the nearest olive trees were growing. They were old with gnarled trunks, but with fertile green branches full of leaves and small flowers, the olives themselves having yet to appear. It was explained that the trees varied in age from twenty to several hundred years old and that the best oil came from the most mature examples. A fact that brought a smile to many of the guests, who appeared mostly retired and of American origin.

The oil would be squeezed from the olives in immaculate stainless-steel machinery. The previous old wood and stone presses had long since been turned into decorative relics in their gardens. The farmers had kept back a supply of olives from the last harvest to demonstrate the process of milling. Verdant green oil flowed from a spout from which small jugs were filled for the tasting. It really was as simple as that. Nothing was added or taken away apart from the stalks, leaves, and stones. This pulp and olive stone by-product was dried and later burned in a stove to provide heat in the winter, with the remnants of oil in this waste making it an excellent fuel.

An hour after they had arrived, the tourists were in the shop deciding how many bottles to take with them. The presentation and packaging were all very modern, with everyone being given the bottles with the English chef on the label, except for Conti. The two bottles he requested were taken from a different box. These had no celebrity chef image; instead, they featured a more traditional design, and the text was in Italian.

"Excuse me, but why have you given me different bottles than the other customers?" he questioned. The young shop assistant looked at him crossly.

"Because you're very clearly Italian and so don't need a label with an English translation, like these Americans. Do you?"

When they were all back on the minibus, Conti stepped on board. He told a white lie and said that he had two bottles of better oil from the oldest trees, but he wanted to compare them to the newer vintages. He asked if anyone was willing to swap one with him. One lady who had bought a case of six agreed enthusiastically. Before he departed, the detective drove his old car around the back of the public car park to where the farmhouse was located. If anyone stopped him, he would claim to have been lost and looking for the exit. A very new-looking Ferrari was parked outside on the drive, spotlessly clean and gleaming red in the late morning sunshine.

It took Conti and Enzo only a few minutes at Conti's hotel to pour samples from the two bottles and see that they were slightly different colours and tasted nothing alike. One smelled of fresh grass and the other of almost nothing at all. The oil, which looked and tasted as they believed it should, boasted Italian labelling. The contents of the bottle labelled in English and featuring the chef's photograph were of dubious origin.

"These are export labels, so it looks like only the English are being conned, making a conviction in Italy more complicated. Do you know anyone in London who you can hand this over to?" Enzo asked his friend.

As an ex-Interpol officer, Conti did have former colleagues in Lyon who could follow up on the UK connection. Still, he was reluctant to let such blatant fakery go entirely unpunished in Italy. He would decide what to do over dinner and act the following day, he told Enzo.

That night, as he was enjoying a digestivo on the hotel terrace and contemplating walking The Duke down to the harbour, a flash of bright red paint went past the dining room windows. A loud, rasping exhaust note followed this. A Ferrari had pulled up at the hotel's front entrance and a woman stepped out of the car before it screeched away again. Conti could only see her back before she disappeared inside the hotel, but he could tell she was young and slim with unusual reddish-blonde hair.

Then it occurred to him that this could be the very same car he had seen parked at the farmhouse earlier that morning. In this case, the girl could be the English chef whose picture was on the bottle. For now, Conti decided to concentrate on figuring out how this fraud was being carried out. The farm was capable of producing the genuine product. According to Enzo, it had been doing so for at least two generations that he was aware of so why suddenly start producing an adulterated product? He needed to know. Then he remembered the briefing document explaining the explosion in UK sales due to the TV chef's endorsement. This answered the question of why. Faced with more demand than they could supply, they were met with a choice between turning away a fortune in additional revenue or bending the rules to fit the new game. The new management had magically sourced some extra olive oil from elsewhere, he concluded.

If the fakes were being bottled and labelled in Seborga as it appeared, the alternative oil must be being brought in somehow. There was only a single-track road to and from the farmhouse. And then he remembered the tanker he had passed going down the hill as he was on his way to the tasting. A call to his friend at the police station narrowed the list of tanker companies down to four within a hundred kilometres along the coast. It then took Enzo only two phone calls to find the company with pale green vehicles like the one Conti had seen.

Enzo had easily extracted the pick-up and drop-off points of that day's journey via Taggia from the company. It transpired there were two different collections with the same final delivery address. Enzo offered to visit the addresses for him, knowing that it would be easier for him to get people to talk when he flashed his badge. He was also interested in learning about the criminal activity occurring on his patch and who was involved. In his experience, crooks rarely stuck to a single criminal activity.

The answer was simple, it turned out. Half the load consisted of Turkish olive oil from a ship that had now departed from Savona, and the remaining space was filled with almond oil sourced from a supplier in Taggia. These were mixed in the one tanker. Neither activity broke any laws in Italy. It was only illegal here if an incorrect label was applied and the product was sold in Italy. Both of these ingredients were considerably cheaper to buy than extra-virgin Taggiasca was to produce. There was also a virtually limitless supply. Each 12,000-litre load was expected to generate over 100,000 euros in extra profit. The tanker company said the last one was the sixth delivery in three months; easily enough for a Ferrari or two, Conti realised.

The following morning, Conti was tearing lumps of salty focaccia and dipping them in his large cup of frothy cappuccino when an English voice behind him asked, "Do you mind my asking? Is salty bread and sweet, creamy coffee a tradition in these parts? I'm a chef and so always curious to learn about new food combinations."

The Italian turned to answer and immediately recognised his fellow diner as Eva Bonetti, the chef from the olive oil label and so, almost certainly, the woman who had been dropped off by the Ferrari the previous night. He guessed that she was perhaps in her early thirties with pale skin from too many long shifts in a dark kitchen. Her mid-length strawberry blonde hair was loosely tied back, showcasing her enormous green eyes. She looked exactly as she did in the photographs, which he had assumed had been tampered with to make her look more attractive.

Conti explained that the tradition of dipping focaccia in coffee was most common in Genoa but could be seen elsewhere in Liguria. "Like the people, it's sweet and sour," he added.

"Like the current fashion for salt and caramel," she offered.

Conti waved over the waiter and ordered more of the fresh focaccia and a cappuccino for her to try. The bread was soft and oily, with visible grains of sea salt scattered on its crust. The coffee was milky and sweet.

"It's delicious" she agreed, making a note on

her phone and taking a photo of herself dipping the bread into the cup for her social media marketing.

The sophisticated Italian warned the Eva not to try this after midday or risk being asked to leave the cafe. Tipping her head to one side and opening her green eyes wide, she asked why this might be so. Conti explained the complicated coffee rituals of his own country, some of which the chef thought made no sense but was willing to accept as fact. This handsome older man seemed to be well-versed in Italian food culture.

Completely surprised by this chance encounter, Conti stalled while he worked out how best to deal with it. Did the pretty young chef now in front of him have anything to do with the fraud that featured her face on the label? Since he had seen her in the Ferrari, he was now suspicious. He would see what he could learn from her while deciding on his next course of action.

She introduced herself and joined him and The Duke at his table to taste the sweet and sour combination. Without asking, the waiter had moved her breakfast place setting to his table while they chatted. The waiter discreetly winked at Conti as he did so. The pair ate their breakfast, and Conti established that she had visited the area before and visited the farm. She already knew a little about the local seafood and pasta. Explaining why she was here for this visit, she told him that it was to have photos taken at the farm for a second cookbook. He then thought of a way to interrogate her at length without causing suspicion.

"I know we've just met, but I'd like to ask an enormous favour. Say no, and I'll completely understand, and that will be the end of the matter."

He explained that his wife had died almost three years earlier and that he had retired from police work when she first fell ill. That night, he was revisiting one of their favourite restaurants, which held many happy memories for them. He told her that it also had the best seafood in Sanremo.

"However, it will be exceedingly difficult for me to enjoy it if I must eat alone. If you were my distraction, you could eat well and perhaps learn more about our traditional local food and wines for your new book. Surely, a double win? "

Although she had already made her plans for that night, she would have been fulfilling them alone. This was a very compelling request from what seemed like a very charming and unthreatening older man – a former police inspector, no less. So, with the start of a tear forming in her green eyes on hearing his sad story, she agreed. Happy that she had accepted without him telling her any lies, Conti was also aware that she would doubtless not be very happy if she ever found the vital part of the story he had left out.

Over a wonderful dinner of baccalà alla Livornese, more Sanremo prawns, clams, and fresh swordfish, he learned that Eva was utterly unaware of anything untoward going on with the oil that was being sold under her name. She also learned from Conti that baccalà could be traced back to the Vikings, Sanremo prawns were the type preferred by three Michelin-starred chef Alain Ducasse, and that swordfish is a sustainable seafood.

Conti had learned that the supplies of oil to the English chef's restaurant were delivered in a box containing five three-litre cans shipped directly from Italy. This separate supply was obviously how the growers ensured she got the genuine product and not the doctored version. Only the supermarket chain received the smaller bottles with the adulterated oil. She told him openly that she earned a modest sum from the oil endorsement, that the restaurant, like most others of its type, ran at a loss, and that most profits came from cookbook sales. She said she drove a ten-year-old Fiat, lived in a rented flat in Earls Court, and her only holiday was coming here to Italy as a guest of the Bruzzones.

Someone was making a fortune from this fraud, but it did not appear to be Eva. After walking back to the hotel along the seafront, they agreed to meet for a cappuccino and focaccia in the morning. Conti went to meet Enzo in a bar near the marina for a nightcap.

Enzo's initial investigation had revealed that both the Turkish oil and the Ferrari had been paid for in cash, which suggested that VAT and income tax had somehow been avoided. This meant the Guardia Finanzia could confiscate the car and impound any fake products still in stock while they investigated that.

Conti asked Enzo to join him and the chef at breakfast the following morning to add legitimacy to the unwelcome news he was about to impart. Before they all met, the two men agreed that after telling her, they could give the Englishwoman a day or two for her to prepare. Only then would Conti pass on his file to former colleagues in London, and the Sanremo police would be handed a copy, along with the Guardia Finanzia in the building next door to them.

Eva strode into the restaurant looking confident and radiant, but her mood quickly changed when she saw the stranger and the serious look on the two men's faces. Conti began by telling her that their original encounter at the hotel was nothing more than an accident. Additionally, it was entirely true that he and his late wife had visited this hotel and Flipper many times. But that was only part of the reason he was here in Sanremo on this occasion. He confessed that he had had an ulterior motive for inviting her to supper.

"Explain," Eva said, now looking highly suspicious.

He told her that, although it was true that he had indeed retired from official police work, he had not told her that he was now investigating food crime and reporting directly to the Italian Prime Minister. His role was to protect indigenous artisan produce by investigating counterfeit food and wines.

"What? You're some type of pasta policeman?" She said non-too flatteringly.

"If you like," he conceded.

Enzo could not help himself from sniggering at this description. "Pasta policeman. Very funny. I like it."

Conti cast his friend a dark look to suggest that this was not a good time for jokes. "Unfortunately, it seems that you may have been dragged unwittingly into such a food fraud."

"Me? What? How?"

"The olive oil you're promoting. While you're serving the real thing at your restaurant, your fans elsewhere are being served a fake oil made from a blend of cheap foreign oil and nut oil.

"No! That's not possible. I've been there and seen the olive trees outside of Seborga."

"I'm sorry, but our colleagues in London have tested the samples. It's true, I'm afraid."

Conti explained that three times as many bottles were being sold as the farm was capable of growing; the numbers did not add up.

"According to the Department of Agriculture, your branded version alone has already sold more this year in the UK than this farm has produced in any year in the last decade."

"Oh shit. But who... how?"

Enzo told her that they did not yet have all the answers but that they were sharing this information with her now because they did not want her to become more involved than she already was.

"You told me they were taking photos of you at the farm, but you don't want to be associated with these people or their produce any further. When this story gets out, it won't look good."

"We wanted to allow you time to make a plan to minimise the damage to your reputation," Conti added.

"Shit!! All those photos those bloody criminals took of me yesterday, smiling like an idiot holding their fake olive oil!"

Conti looked at Enzo, hoping he had something encouraging to say to her, but he didn't.

Eva continued thinking out loud. "My good name. My Michelin star. My restaurant! Ruined for the price of a few holidays. Why didn't I just stick to cooking?"

Although now, even with tears streaming down her pretty face, Conti decided there was little point in her wallowing in self-pity. There were important things for her to do, and she needed to pull herself together.

"Unfortunately, Eva, this world is full of crooks, and this was your time to find that out – the hard way. Now, you need to move quickly to limit the damage. Enzo and I have given this some thought and have some suggestions."

Eva was only just realising that Conti must have known about this when he invited her to dinner, but said nothing. She was now scared, all alone in a foreign country and looking for someone to hit out at.

"You've been eating meals with me for two days, but waited until now to tell me this. That's devious. Is that even legal?"

"We knew certain things, but only just received confirmation of our suspicions last night." Enzo backed up his friend by confirming he had just given Conti the news from London.

"What Conti says is true. You can still take the initiative."

"Initiative? It sounds like it's already way out of control to me."

Although it might be painful, Enzo argued that

going in front of the UK media to break the news to her fans and customers would be better than the alternative.

"If your tabloid newspapers get this first, they'll hang you out to dry. If you move first, you'll at least control the agenda and could paint yourself as another victim of the scammers."

"You think? People will buy that?"

"You can say that as soon as you found out the truth, you've come clean and will make things right. Paint yourself as much a victim of this as the consumers. Which, in fact, you are."

He said that he believed the retailers should have done more due diligence on the product and would have little choice but to remove all products from the shelves and refund any customers who requested one. He added that, although this might not be great, it was the least worst outcome. For Eva, it was still a bitter pill to swallow when everything had been going so well for her.

"Two men in as many days have conned me," she said bitterly.

"Two men?" Enzo quizzed.

Eva cast a look at Conti who sprang to his own defence.

"Mine was merely a case of being economical with information until I knew it was a fact," he argued. "We just need a few more days to get everything in place before we confront the villains.

Then we can go public in a coordinated way."

"A few more days?!" Anger was now replacing Eva's self-pity. "No way! I'm going to make a few calls as soon as I get home and stir things up. Lots of senior journalists and TV personalities dine at my restaurant. They always ask me to get them a table that I don't have at the last minute. I've got plenty of favours I can call in. I might hold a press conference tomorrow that'll make Casa Bruzzone choke on their focaccia!"

Conti pleaded for caution. "If they're warned before we're ready, they might destroy evidence or even flee, and there'll be no justice."

Under the table, apparently, sensing the rising tensions, The Duke gave a short bark to remind everyone he was there.

Seemingly determined to make Conti feel guilty, Eva added, "I hope you're ashamed of getting The Duke involved with this deception."

Hearing his name, The Duke looked up, head cocked to one side. Eva stormed out angrily, saying nothing more.

Their police contacts in London had been trying to trace the shipments into the UK back to their origin. They had been shipped from somewhere in Italy to Harwich, they were told.

"We really do need those extra days to tie up all these loose ends." Enzo underlined.

"As the nearest large port, I guessed they would

ship the bottles out from Genoa so I put a call in to our old friend at the Genoa Port Authority. He didn't answer, but I've left a voicemail."

Conti's phone rang, and he looked at the screen to see that it was a video call. He nodded to Enzo. "It's Roberto from Genoa."

"Roberto, Ciao! I'm here with Enzo. I'll put you on speaker."

Vittorio propped up the phone on the table so they all could see each other. "Is the old team back together again?" Roberto said, laughing.

Enzo greeted him with, "Roberto, please do the rest of us a favour and swallow some ugly pills."

"Ha! You already ate them all!"

Getting to the point, Conti ended the levity. "Roberto, I have a favour to ask."

"Not an official request, I take it?

"Not yet, at least."

Conti told him that he would send some shipment details via WhatsApp and asked him to check if that load had originated from Genoa, look for names, addresses, dates, and any other information he could find out about who was behind it.

"Would this request have anything to do with a rumoured new job you have? I hear they're calling you the Dining Detective at Genoa police station."

"Ha. That's rich. I'd be surprised if there are

any detectives remaining at Genoa police station who haven't suffered a heart attack from overindulging in lunches paid for by those seeking favours from them. They don't catch many crooks but could find a free meal in the blink of an eye."

Roberto laughed and told him he would see what he could find out and signed off, saying, "We must meet up again, guys! Dinner in Genoa with the Dining Detective?"

"Soon. I owe you," Conti concluded.

"No. I still owe you more. And I don't forget." Roberto told him.

Conti pocketed his mobile phone and stood to leave, telling Enzo that he needed to go and talk to Eva before she spilled the story to anyone who would listen.

"Maybe it was a mistake to forewarn her?" Enzo reflected.

"I think she'll see sense," Conti assured him.

At the reception desk, Conti asked for Eva's room number but was told that she had already checked out.

"I phoned for a taxi to the airport not five minutes ago. She seemed somewhat upset." the receptionist told him.

She could still be outside, Conti realised. He ran out and down to the front steps, where a driver was loading Eva's luggage into the boot of his taxi.

"Eva, please wait!"

"Why? So, that you can tell me more lies?"

Conti caught up with her and reached as if to take her arm, but then thought better of it.

"You must appreciate that I couldn't say anything to you until I was sure you weren't involved in the scam." Eva was now even more shocked. It had never occurred to her that she might also be a suspect.

"What! Me? Involved?! You suspected me?! This nightmare just gets worse."

"How could I know you weren't until I'd checked you out?"

Eva furiously slumped like a child having a tantrum onto the rear seat of the taxi, slamming the door behind her. As he stood watching the taxi disappear into the mid-morning traffic, Conti received another call from Roberto.

"Roberto. That was quick."

"Well, our port handlers prefer to deal with enquiries from headquarters quickly on the phone. They don't want management to go down on the docks in person and inspect the cargo and paperwork. It's like their own little kingdom down there."

He told him that there had been three shipments of the olive oil to Harwich so far this year, and five more to New Jersey.

"New Jersey, as in New York?! Are you sure it's the same people?"

"Yes, and the weight of the American shipments was heavier than those to London. I'll send the figures."

"And did you get the name of the person responsible for receiving the shipment in the States?" Conti asked.

"Bruno - wait a minute - Bruzzone!"

"Now that's very interesting! You're a star, Roberto! Got to run!"

Vittorio hung up, checked his phone and saw he had a voicemail from Enzo. He pressed the play button.

The message said, "I've just learnt that the American, Candice McKinley, has been in Italy for somewhere in the region of twenty months. They're not married, although they are indeed partners in other ways. There are also some local reports that she often refers to herself as Candice Bruzzone. She's outstayed her visa for a year and a half."

The next morning, Conti received a text message from Eva. She must have calmed down and reflected on the events of the previous twenty-four hours. She told him she would prepare but not act on an announcement until she heard from them that they were ready. She also promised to send a draft of any press release before it was issued. Nothing more. Conti was relieved to receive this news and to know that his trust in her had not been misplaced.

Squashed into his Alfa Romeo, Conti and Enzo followed a marked police car on the drive up the mountain to Seborga. Both cars pulled up beside the Ferrari and the Range Rover at the olive farm. Accompanied by two uniformed officers, they approached the farmhouse. There, a group, including Fabio Bruzzone and Candice McKinley, was having drinks on a front-facing terrace. They all appeared perplexed by the arrival of the group. After first holding up his police ID, Enzo addressed the group.

"I am sorry to interrupt your aperitivo, but Miss McKinley needs to pack a small bag and go with these officers."

Candice stood up from the table and took two paces toward the edge of the terrace.

"I don't know who you think you are, but you must be joking! I'm an American citizen. I'm going nowhere without speaking to my Embassy and my lawyer."

Enzo smiled and continued, "Earlier today, the American Consulate in Genoa was made aware of our visit and why we were coming to speak to you. They were offered the opportunity to attend but declined."

Fabio Bruzzone now stood looking confused. "Can someone explain to me exactly what's happening here?"

"Don't say a word. They can't prove anything." McKinley quickly interjected. Bruzzone now appeared even more confused.

"Prove? What is there to prove?

Conti had stayed behind the police officers and now looked down at The Duke and whispered, "If he's acting innocent, he's very good at it."

The Duke barked.

Enzo told them that soon, a press statement would be released online by Eva Bonetti in London, removing her endorsement of their olive oil. It would apologise to the customers who had been conned by them and thereby expose their criminal activities on the farm.

Bruzzone was now beginning to get annoyed.

"Who exactly has been conned? How? We sell our oil with her face on the bottle in the UK, and she gets a cut. What's wrong with that?"

Enzo shook his head.

"What's wrong is that UK customers are getting cheap Turkish olive oil labelled as Italian Taggiasca."

Bruzzone's face was now red with rage, "That's complete nonsense!"

McKinley asked, "Even if this outrageous accusation was true, if this is happening in the UK, exactly what does that have to do with the Italian police?"

Bruzzone now turned to McKinley. "Why are

you even countenancing the idea that this could be true? Why would we sell foreign oil when we have the real thing right here? After we ran out of last year's crop, you did turn down those new orders from the supermarkets for more, didn't you?"

Now it was McKinley's turn to look furious. "I thought I told you to keep your mouth shut before you get us all arrested."

Conti stepped forward, The Duke at his side. "I work for the Italian government, exposing food and wine fraud. These uniformed officers are enforcing a warrant for an immigration violation by Miss McKinley."

McKinley had calmed down and looked self-assured once more. "They have no jurisdiction, Fabio. They're just trying to scare us into confessing to something we haven't done."

"That's just not possible because we haven't done anything!" he replied.

Conti told them that they did not need a confession concerning what they had been doing. He had all the evidence in the folder, which he waved at them. He removed a few of the sheets from the file.

"Logs of shipments of cheap olive oil received from Turkey. An invoice for nut oil from Savona was delivered to Seborga. All payments are made in cash without VAT being added. But the most interesting are those from Genoa to someone called Bruzzone in the USA."

"That's crazy! Why would I ship anything to myself when I'm here?

"Perhaps there is someone else called Bruzzone, and it's just a coincidence." Enzo proposed, joking.

Conti smiled. "It seems that there is another Bruzzone involved in this fraud, but we'll get to that in a moment."

Conti continued to detail the analysis of the fake oil shipped, which confirmed it to be a Turkish olive oil blended with nut oil. Then he told them that they had obtained a file from the EU giving the number of olive trees on this farm signed by Signore Bruzzone and the estimated volume of oil that those were likely to produce.

Enzo turned to Conti, asking, "And does the oil shipped under the Bruzzone label match with the volume it would be possible for that number of trees to produce?"

"I think everyone here knows the answer to that. It does not." Conti answered.

Bruzzone seemed exasperated with everything he had to take in. "I don't know about any of this. What the fuck has been going on around here?"

Meanwhile, the two unknown guests had been listening and looking increasingly alarmed. They now stood and began to leave without explanation or apology. As one of them approached the officers he said, "I certainly didn't know anything about this. I was about to place a large order. Their oil is fake? Unbelievable!"

"Most of it is." He confirmed. "You're both free to leave."

McKinley tried to persuade them to stay, "No, wait! I can explain and clear all of this up when we get rid of these clowns."

Enzo told her, "The only clown leaving this circus today is you. As an American citizen..."

He was interrupted by McKinley, "Oh, finally, an acknowledgement that I have rights as an American."

"The problem is that you have no rights as an Italian. As a foreign national, you're entitled to stay in Italy for only 90 days at a time. You've been here for nearly two years. You've outstayed your welcome in every possible sense."

"I'm here living with my Italian boyfriend. This is his house. We're a couple. We'll get married."

Enzo shook his head again.

"If he had been your husband, you may have been allowed to apply for residency, but as it is, that's too late."

Conti took out another document. He explained that this contained the address in Palm Springs that McKinley had given on entry to Italy. Moreover, it was the same address listed on the paperwork for the oil shipped into the USA.

"What American shipments?" What address?" Bruzzone asked, now almost in tears. "I sent one load of olive oil to London which, as far as I know, came from this farm. I know nothing about American shipments or this Turkish oil!"

Now it was Conti's turn to shake his head, this time in dismay rather than disbelief. "It is becoming increasingly clear that you know very little about what is going on around here, Signore Bruzzone. But ignorance is not a defence in the eyes of the law. Maybe you spent too much time playing with that fancy boat and car instead of keeping an eye on what was going on here. Neither of those vehicles belongs to you, incidentally."

"They were gifts from my fiancé!" he replied petulantly.

"Very generous, but they were bought by a company in which Miss McKinley has a fifty per cent stake."

"Well, there you are; the other fifty is mine. She bought them through the business. What's wrong with that?"

"It is true that the other director and shareholder does have your surname." Conti conceded.

"I told you!" Bruzzone said, thinking that at last, he was regaining some control.

"Unfortunately, for you, the Christian name is

different. The other director is your brother, Bruno who, interestingly, has the same address in Palm Springs as your fiancé provided. He is also the co-signatory on their company's American bank account."

Fabio Bruzzone was finally beginning to piece together all the bits of information that had been raining down on him. He was arriving at the inevitable conclusion that he had also been conned. Worse still, it was his own brother and the woman he thought loved him who had crushed him. He was close to tears.

The hard-faced McKinley said, "Look, this is all very interesting, but we've already established that I'm going home, where my real lover and huge sums of money are waiting for me. So, if there's nothing else, I'll say ciao."

The two police officers moved forward and served their deportation warrant. Candice McKinley feigned boredom. The officers told her that they would give her a few minutes to pack a bag before taking her to the airport and escorting her on board a flight to New York. Enzo added that her passport would be stamped 'deported' and she would likely never be allowed back into the EU.

McKinley kicked the table, spilling the wine glasses.

"So, what! It's like the Third World here anyway! You can't get a decent hot shower or a coffee bigger than an egg cup, and who even likes fucking olive oil anyway?"

Now it was Conti's turn to be angry. He raged, "People like you think of this as some sort of victimless white-collar crime, but it's not! When criminals like you bypass rules designed to protect the public, people can become ill or even die! You have no idea what they were adding to those bottles, nor did you care! You've also risked ruining the career of a hardworking chef who may never recover from this catastrophe."

McKinley fumed quietly.

"What about me?" Fabio asked his partner.

"What about you? You're a pathetic child who couldn't run an ice cream stall on a packed beach in August, never mind an international business. Your brother is twice the man you are. In every respect."

Fabio Bruzzone sat down, looking stunned and broken.

Enzo thought now was a good time for their coup de grâce.

"Ah, yes, brother Bruno. Well, it turns out that as well as sharing a bed and a criminal business with Miss McKinley, they both share a residency problem."

Candice and Fabio look puzzled.

Enzo explained that on checking, Bruno had arrived in America on a student visa, later obtaining an extension for an internship but that had run out and he, too, was an illegal immigrant, only in case in the USA.

He paused for a moment to let all this sink in.

"US immigration officers raided the address in Palm Springs today. They've taken away the paperwork, computers, and some cash, and Bruno Bruzzone is in handcuffs. He is, as we speak, on his way to New York."

Enzo had not finished. "Well, as long as I'm here, it seems that some other laws have been broken in Italy, and the proceeds of crime are forfeit to the state. Foreign nationals can't own cars or boats registered in Italy. So, I'd like the keys to both, if you please," he said, looking at Fabio Bruzzone.

Fabio slowly fished out a key ring from his pocket while McKinley sneered at them all.

"What do I care? When Bruno and I get married, I'll send you a photo of us together, leaving the wedding in the new Ferrari he took delivery of this week!" McKinley told Fabio, driving the dagger even further into the wound.

"Ah, that's going to be a bit difficult for you," Conti told her. "Because while you're being placed on a plane to the USA, Bruno will be on a flight back to Italy. His passport will also be stamped 'deported,' so he'll never return to the USA. You might be able to snatch one last look at each other somewhere over the Atlantic."

Enzo added, "One more thing, the FBI has been informed of your international scam and has copies of all these documents as well as the ones US immigration confiscated today."

Conti waved his file of papers again.

"So, I expect that you'll find a little reception committee waiting for you at US passport control, Miss McKinley. You could be there for a while. I'd take a good book to read. Try 'Extra Virgin' by Annie Hawes. I liked it a lot."

"Look at that mangy mongrel," McKinley shouted, pointing beyond the officers.

Conti turned to see The Duke peeing on a wheel of her Range Rover

"Fucking perfect! You Europeans and your barbaric bathroom habits. I'll be glad to get back to civilisation."

Eva had not fared too badly from the coverage the press release had generated. Her regular diners who worked in the media had undoubtedly helped in positioning her as a second victim. The upside was that her brand had been exposed to a vast audience, and she was selling more cookbooks. In the following days, Enzo had been able to pass Eva the details of another local olive-growing family with impeccable credentials and a high-quality Taggiasca oil. The new supplier stated that they could have a replacement oil on the market the following year.

"They say there's only news and no such thing as bad publicity," Conti said to Enzo, trying to make them both feel less guilty for pursuing this matter.

Eva had time to reflect and came to realise that Conti had done her a favour. After all, he did not have to say anything to her. She only discovered the truth when she read about it in the media, like everyone else. However, she had not shown any gratitude when he first shared the news with her. She felt betrayed. However, if the UK police had moved to stop the fraud before she had time to prepare, she would have appeared complicit in the whole sad affair. Her career would have been over, and her brand name would have been ruined.

Several months later, Conti was in Venezia looking into a vast prosecco scam when he received a WhatsApp message from the English chef. It was a photograph of a page from an open cookbook. The dish was entitled Pasta Conti with Sanremo red prawns. On the page was a handwritten message. It read, 'I survived. I named this dish after you. Slightly fishy but sweet under the shell.' A second WhatsApp said: 'This copy has been posted to you. There's a table for you in London, any time. Ciao xxx'

Chapter 14: Bogus Barolo

It had been her idea to have a video call. It had been several months since Conti had spoken to Elena, and he had not seen her in person since Paola's funeral. Conti's initial research had provided no clue as to where to begin this new investigation, so he had sent a wine label he had received to her home address in Lyon. When the video call connected, Conti was shocked at what he saw. "You've changed from white to red! What happened?"

"I got bored with the white bob. The spooks here had started to take me for granted, so I thought I'd spice things up."

Conti smiled. He did admire her anti-establishment attitude. "It's very red."

"They call it Vampire Blood Red. I thought appropriate for an Eastern European."

"You mean you thought it would rattle the cages of your bosses."

"That's an enjoyable side effect."

The former Interpol colleagues spent a few more minutes catching up on their current circumstances, both deliberately avoiding mention of their last face-to-face meeting at the funeral.

"Anyway, I've been reading about you in the media."

"How so?" Conti replied, puzzled.

Elena explained that her algorithm had identified food crimes and picked up an online version of a Rome newspaper column about a gastronome with a gun.

"It doesn't mention you by name, but the writer appears to be aware of your mission, and she discusses you with some enthusiasm."

"Enzo told me that some woman from Rome had called him asking questions. Sounds like the same person."

"She sees you as a masked crusader righting the wrongs perpetrated on Italian food and wine makers. So, then I thought that if you're Batman, that must make Enzo Robin. Since then, I've not been able to get the image of the jovial, tubby Enzo in tights with his pants on the outside, out of my head."

Conti laughed along with her saying, "So, you don't think this woman is trouble, and she's not going to unmask me?"

Elena told him that she would be surprised if

that were to happen. The journalist gave the impression of being a supporter, not a detractor, that she would know that secrecy and anonymity were his best weapons.

"I think she just sees this as an interesting story and a good cause. And she's right. The way she tells it is fun and quite glamorous. I wouldn't be surprised if she doesn't already know your identity, has seen your photo, and sees that you're a bit of a catch. She wants to keep that to herself."

"Now, you're getting carried away, Elena."

"She could, however, also turn into a superfan stalker."

"That's enough. What about my wine label?"

Elena told him that she had tested the paper and ink used on the printed labels of the fake Barolo and compared it to a genuine sample. They were identical in every way. This was unusual. Labels were usually copies, often good ones, but fakes, nonetheless. Conti told her that even more puzzling was that the bottles, corks, and foil all appeared to be of the correct origin. That only the contents of the bottles were incorrect.

"I think this is a particularly clever scam," Conti told her. "The genuine product is sold at very high value in small quantities and seldom consumed at the point of purchase, if at all."

Conti added with a grudging hint of admiration for their cunning, "They could have put cheap plonk in the bottles, but they didn't. They used a perfectly acceptable wine made from Nebbiolo grapes in more or less the same region, but costing a fraction of the price. This gave them some level of insurance against getting found out too quickly."

He explained that only if expert buyers opened the bottles would they know they had been conned. However, most of these bottles were bought as investments by inexperienced buyers and then stored in dark cellars to be traded later, usually for a good profit. Even a buyer uncorking one to drink on a special occasion would need to be a connoisseur to distinguish the real thing from the twenty-euro Nebbiolo that was in the bottle. Most of those sorts of buyers were not. Any number of casual, entrepreneurial investors, often with delusions of grandeur, dabbled in the fine wine market. The thieves were making a twenty-thousand-euro profit on every case they faked.

"Then this looks like an inside job," Elena suggested.

"So, it would appear." Conti acknowledged.

The drive to Bra near Barolo from Genoa took three hours. It could have been driven in two, but Conti insisted on using the Alfa Romeo. So, just in time for lunch, he pulled into the courtyard of Cantine Lorenzon in the ancient Piedmont town of Bra. Home to Italy's University of Gastronomic

Science, The Slow Food Movement, and the annual International White Truffle Fair, Bra has no shortage of great places to eat. It is also at the centre of a region that includes some of the world's best wine-growing locations. Samples of these wines can be tasted at the Banco del Vino, located underneath the University.

However tempting the menu, Conti knew he had to show restraint. The Bernardi family, whose Barolo had been faked, had invited him to dine with them that night at the winery. He felt sure that with their family pedigree, it would be a dinner to remember. An introduction had been arranged for him as a wine marketing expert doing research for the government with the aim of boosting sales abroad so the Bernardis accepted him without question.

Meeting the three generations of the family running the business over dinner provided no real clues as to who might be responsible or why. They all stood to lose equally in both the short and long term from the undermining of their family product. A teenage cousin who had joined the workforce on a trial basis was also present. He was told that the boy's father had begged his brother-in-law to take him on after completing school; he refused to go to university despite having no other career plans.

Head down, looking at his phone, the boy

appeared to be as reluctant to be there with them as he had been to continue his education. His father and uncle just hoped he would grow out of it. The Bernardi's teenage daughter was similarly engrossed in her phone, typing furiously with two fingers. Suddenly, they both stood up and asked to be excused. By the time the dessert dishes had been cleared away, only the older adults remained at the table for pecorino cheese, cherries, and grappa.

The winery's bottles and foils were bought from a wholesaler to whom anyone had access and they sold foils to hundreds of small wineries right across northern Italy. The labels had been sourced locally from a traditional small printer they had trusted for over fifty years. They only ordered what they needed for each year, counting then storing any leftover labels in a wooden cabinet. Although hardly high security, it was difficult to see how any meaningful quantity could get into the hands of the crooks without the family knowing they were missing.

Attention turned back to the person who had reported the first fake bottle. They had purchased it through a dealer who had sold it on behalf of a third party in Stuttgart. The fake had been spotted when the eventual owner opened one bottle at a special dinner. Along with other fine wine collectors, each had brought a different bottle to taste and share. One, and then another of these experts present called into question the provenance of the Barolo thus triggering this investigation.

Inferring official police credentials that he no longer had, Conti extracted the contact details from the wine merchant who had acted as an intermediary for the German buyer and seller. The trail led full circle back to a tasting at the Bernardi winery. The German buyer had acquired two cases following a wine tasting there two years earlier. Surely the family was not faking its own wine, Conti asked himself. Perhaps they were greedy, but they could not grow enough grapes to meet demand. After all, this wine had DOC status. The land where it could be produced was finite and could not be expanded by so much as a metre.

"Could they have large debts or other money problems?" Conti wondered.

The family appeared to be enjoying a comfortable yet modest lifestyle. There were two cars, both over ten years old, parked outside. A van with the name on its sides of an even older vintage was parked near the winery. There were no apparent signs of excess, he concluded.

Franco Bernardi told him that an aristocratic woman from Rome had run regular Barolo tours and wine tastings a dozen times a year over the past five years. They were pricy and lavish affairs, consisting of visits to the vineyards and winery tours targeting wealthy foreigners. Later, a five-course dinner of local delicacies was paired with excellent vintages of five of the best wines from the Bernardi's private cellar. They attracted small groups of foodies and wine collectors from all over Europe, America, and Asia. The family was paid generously for supplying the wine and hosting the events. They had built a good relationship with the organiser.

Several months after attending such an event, the German buyer had received an email. It stated that someone had paid a deposit for an order for several cases of the Barolo a year before its production. That wine had now been harvested and bottled, but the buyer could not be contacted to pay the balance and accept delivery. Instead, these were being offered to selected individuals on the mailing list at last year's pre-harvest price. This was still a substantial sum, but it seemed like a good investment in something rare and sought after, which had already started to appreciate.

When Conti visited her, the attractive Italian in her thirties who ran the tours acknowledged that, other than those guests who had ticked the box to opt out, their names and email addresses were entered into a database.

Furthermore, this information had later been purchased by a third-party data broker.

"Presumably for marketing relevant products," she added.

"Such as fine wines?" Conti suggested, probing for a reaction.

She nodded. "I wouldn't know for sure, but I guess so, and maybe luxury cruises, designer wristwatches, and so on. Data sharing is a normal modern business practice, as I'm sure you're well aware."

Conti knew from experience he would have difficulty even finding a physical address for this data broker, let alone obtaining any meaningful information from them about its use. They were notoriously sensitive to growing data protection legislation and so secretive about their activity. His momentary hot lead had gone very cold. If it was not the family and the tasting company was running a legitimate related business, as they seemed to have been doing for years, who did that leave, he asked himself.

Conti decided that he needed a good dinner and some Piedmont wine as fuel for his thoughts. Back at the hotel, he skipped through the folder provided in the room with local information, looking for a restaurant in which to spend the evening. Amongst the flyers in the plastic sleeves was one advertising the wine-tasting events at The Bernardi Winery. Checking the website, he discovered one was scheduled for the coming weekend.

Having booked at short notice and arriving unannounced on the evening of the tasting in a dark suit and crisp white shirt, Conti appeared overdressed compared to the American and northern European guests. Conti only wore Armani. His wife had worked for the famous brand throughout her career and had chosen all her husband's wardrobe. He had not bought a new suit since she died.

As the family had invited him to be their guest the day before, the organiser could hardly refuse without either looking suspicious or rude. An extra place was set for him at the table. In front of each place setting was what he assumed was a menu. It was, in fact, a brochure with a glossy cover detailing the wines to be tasted that evening, a blank sheet on the reverse for writing tasting notes.

Above each wine was an actual-size replica of the bottle label. The woman explained to her guests that the brochure was a memento to keep as a reminder of their trip. The detective joined in the tasting and enjoyed his pasta dinner with truffles, followed by roast lamb. He was relaxed, chatting with the family, the gregarious hostess, and her interesting guests.

"What did you think of the Barolo?" the organiser asked.

"I think the 2009 was the perfect pairing for the white truffle risotto."

"You seem knowledgeable about your wine and what goes well with it."

"I would know if it was genuine if that's what you mean," Conti replied, probing.

"Oh really, and how would you know? What would give it away?"

"A good mature Barolo would have started off ruby red but become more orange in colour while remaining translucent when held to the light, as this one does. This taste always reminds me of eating Ferrero Rocher with good Illy espresso. A great combination."

"Well, chocolate, hazelnuts, and coffee are all flavours associated with that wine, so you're quite correct."

The ex-policeman told her that his father had trained at The Splendido Hotel in Portofino. He described his father as a sponge for culinary knowledge who soaked up all he could from the sommeliers and chefs who worked at those places. He explained that, as he was ultimately responsible for purchasing fine wines and other expensive ingredients that his wealthy guests expected, this knowledge was invaluable.

"My father told me he could sniff out con men and chancers amongst his suppliers long before he found their dubious products. I eventually learned that what he meant was that bad people were sometimes easier to spot than bad products. He taught me all he knew about both people and food. This wine, however, tastes entirely genuine and is very good indeed."

Meanwhile, the untethered Duke was wandering around scavenging for pieces of anti-pasta by tapping guests' shoes with his right paw. Sometimes, he only received a head scratch but occasionally a piece of prosciutto or some other tasty morsel. Then he took cheese from the event's organiser but growled at the Bernardi's young cousin who offered a mere morsel of focaccia.

Witnessing this, the attractive hostess jokingly suggested to Conti, "A pure carnivore. He's not interested in bread. He just wants meat."

Conti shook his head as if to admonish the dog's behavior.

"The Duke likes to think he is a great judge of character and my guardian against those he dislikes. However, I'm sure that if the young man had offered a sausage rather than bread, he'd have overlooked any initial reservations."

Conti could not help but feel that this young man had something to hide. His relationship with the other family members was awkward. Moreover, The Duke didn't like him. Despite this, he felt that he was just too naive and inexperienced to have anything to do with a fraud of this sophistication, and Conti discounted him.

The woman laughed aloud at Conti's joke about The Duke. She then squeezed his arm in the familiar way old friends might. He could not help but feel that the beautiful younger woman was paying slightly too much attention to a man at least twenty years her senior, clearly still wearing his wedding ring.

The following day, Conti visited the small printer in Bra that had provided the Bernardi labels for two generations. The old, dark workshop smelled of machine oil, ink, and paper dust. Stacks of fading printed paper were piled on every flat surface, an unwanted record of events, sales efforts, parties, and weddings long passed. If there was any inventory system, it appeared to be in complete chaos. From the corner of his eye, through one of the few uncluttered windows, Conti spotted the young Bernardi cousin making what he was sure was a very indiscreet drug purchase at the side of the railway station. His attention was brought back to the matter at hand by the return of the printer from his back office.

"Si, we print the brochure for the Senorina. Si. She wanted the labels to look exactly the same as the wine bottles, so we used the same printing plates and paper to make the background colour identical. That made life very easy for us as we had all the materials to hand. She was very pleased."

"And the size of the order?"

"How many did we make? I would have to check my records. The first brochure was a few years ago, and there have been two updated versions since then."

When he returned, Conti was stunned by the printer's reply. "You didn't think three thousand of each run was a large number of brochures for local wine tastings?"

"Signore, surely you've ordered printed products before? All the work is in preparing the artwork and setting up the plates. Once the press is running, the difference between hundreds and thousands is only five minutes and a few euros' worth of paper. Look around you at all these overruns. As I always do, I provided her with prices for a range of quantities, from 300 to 3,000. Most people take more than they think they need because it costs so little extra. You want me to complain because she spends a little more money?"

The detective did the mental arithmetic. Each brochure contained five exact copies of labels. They were printed on the same old printing press, using the same paper and inks. When cut out of the brochures, fifteen thousand wine labels had unwittingly been handed to the fraudsters. Even if they had given away 150 brochures per year to their tasting clients, they were still looking at the potential for €25 million worth of fake wine. What was unknown was how many had already been applied to bottles containing cheaper Nebbiolo. The answer, he believed, he would never find out. However, it was highly likely that many people worldwide had already been conned. They already unknowingly had fakes in their wine collections, which they thought were genuine bottles of Bernardi Reserve Barolo. Most would probably never know.

This was a well-established local supply network with growers using the same suppliers for generations. After a few days of visiting other wineries in the region from a list acquired from the bottle makers, Conti discovered that the counterfeiters had found their supplier of Nebbiolo not too far away. They already had the same glass bottles, as well as the corks and foils, as the Bernardis. This, presumably, was why they had been chosen. Notably, the Nebbiolo winery was located outside the DOC region for Barolo, so this much younger wine could be purchased wholesale for about ten euros a bottle. Yet, being of the grape variety, it had the correct colour and bouquet. It would be sufficient to fool most non-experts who would expect it to be the genuine article. All the fraudsters had to do was steam off the labels and replace them with their own cut that were from the surplus brochures. Conti had to admit it was a smart but simple scheme.

But the dilemma Conti now faced was how best to break up the fake supply chain and limit the damage to the Barolo name. Whilst a prosecution in this case would alert those unknowingly conned, those people were unlikely to recover any money. They would probably be happier in their ignorance than to see their investment declared worthless. The publicity would also damage all trust in the family label, undermining existing genuine stock and future years' production. And somewhere out there were hundreds of labels that had yet to be used. He had his case solved. He just needed to decide his next move.

Like most detectives, Conti hated coincidences. He could not help but wonder if there was a connection between seeing the young Bernardi cousin and his dealer so close to the printer of the labels. In the absence of any more leads to follow, he decided to seek out the young man and confront him. He returned to the vineyard on the pretence of buying a few bottles of Barolo to take home. Parking away from the main house, he took a stroll around the nearby buildings. As he passed the small bottling shed, redundant at this time of year, he caught a smell he immediately recognised.

Backtracking, he tried the door and found it unlocked. Inside, in the half-light, he could just see the daughter of the Bernardi family and her cousin struggling to get back into their jeans. On the floor was what looked like a stubbed-out marihuana joint that was still smouldering. Conti had left the door ajar so he could see what was going on, and the young man, who was now dressed to his waist, dashed for the opening.

Conti's well-placed left foot sent the boy sprawling. As soon as he hit the ground, The Duke was in his face, growling as if he might bite his nose. The girl continued to fasten the buttons of her shirt, looking largely unconcerned about what was taking place. The former policeman now realised that the reason for the young man's discomfort around his uncle and other male cousins had nothing to do with the fake wine.

"The Duke and I are going back into town for lunch, after which we'll drive back here to buy some wine from your uncle. I hope he then tells me that you've left suddenly and gone home without explanation. Otherwise, I'll have a sad tale to impart to him and to your enormous male cousins." He picked up the joint the boy had dropped, sniffed it, and added. "Do we understand each other?" The two nodded, and he turned and left them to say their goodbyes.

Having pieced together all the clues and thought it through, it was clear that what was happening had been taking place for some time. Blowing the whistle now and having the one person arrested would resolve little. On the contrary, it would undoubtedly forewarn any co-conspirators who might not even be in Italy. This gang had invested in marketing materials and spent months recruiting wealthy guests to tastings then they waited several more months before making their sting with the email offer. These fraudsters were patiently playing the long game. Their pursuer perhaps needed to do the same and keep the cork in the bottle for now. The Government Special Investigator would call his employers in Rome the following day with a proposal.

It took several weeks for Conti to arrange phone taps to track all the threads leading from the Bernardi fraud to the fellow felons. Then, a couple more weeks passed while the necessary court orders were put in place, allowing the authorities to implement their own sting. Four suspects were located at different locations, and with Conti confronting the person he had identified as the ringleader in Rome, a carefully coordinated action began to target the others.

"Remember me?" Conti asked, looking his most profound. The woman hesitated but finally began to recognise his face.

"You came to the wine tasting in September. The mysterious marketing man with his little dog."

At first, her mouth began to turn up at the corners to form a smile, but then quickly inverted as she grew suspicious at seeing him again in Rome. Conti held his phone screen up for the woman to view. Live video was streaming showing her Maserati Cielo Spider in mid-air as it was being craned into a tow truck. Struck dumb, she merely clasped her head in her hands.

"Pearlescent white with red leather – nice colour combination, by the way."

Before she could recover from the shock, Conti clicked another link on his phone to show a video of Guardia di Finanza police officers fastening a large padlock to the front door of her house in the fashionable Trastevere district of Rome.

"The officers have removed eighteen designer handbags, six Swiss watches, twenty-three pairs of shoes, and a couple of pieces of artwork, one of which may or may not be a genuine Banksy. These are being treated as the proceeds of a crime until it can be proven otherwise. A similar raid also co-occurred at your lakeside villa in Como and your seaside apartment in Amalfi. If it makes you feel any better, all your comrades in crime are also enduring the same fate this morning in Milan and Bologna."

The woman looked like she was about to vomit. All the colour had drained from her face. However, she still could not speak. She did not need to ask why this was happening. One of her partners had previously begged her to quit while they were ahead and move on. They had spent three years making millions of euros every year. He argued that they were pushing their luck too far. She could see now that she had been too greedy.

Conti continued, "All your credit and debit cards have been deactivated. And there's a lady police officer here with me with a warrant to take your passport. If you have any cash on you, you can keep that, as you might need it to get a bus or train to any friends or family you have left. Once we've calculated what we believe you've defrauded, we'll propose a settlement for you to make reparations. However, we estimate the process could take several years, so don't wait by the phone. Oh, and that reminds me, the officer also needs your iPhone."

Chapter 15: Strange Bedfellows

Elena called. "Have you seen her latest column?"

"Who? What column?"

Elena explained that she had been following the column written by Claudia Russo in Rome. "She's good. Her writing is funny and smart."

"It's great that you've found something interesting to read while you should be working."

"She's made you a direct challenge. Russo claims that she's found a new case of fake food and dares you to investigate it. It could be a trap, of course. She might lure you to a dungeon and handcuff you to a bed," his former colleague joked.

"This isn't a game. Some of these people are dangerous."

One of Russo's readers had sent in a photo of a tin of premium-branded, ground coffee with a dead cockroach inside. When the reader complained to the manufacturer, they said the barcode number on the can was a fake. They had already received other complaints about cans of coffee carrying their brand that they had not produced. The genuine manufacturers had researched the contents of one can and found an insect only found in East Asia. They suspected that the fakes were probably from China and were being sold through street markets and cut-price grocery stores. The premium coffee, costing seven euros per can, fit the pattern of other products being faked, but this was the first time Conti had encountered this scam.

Although, at first, he thought the commercial value of this scam was less than that of bigger ticket items such as Franciacorta, the potential volume and broad reach of its customer base could make it enormous. Conti set up the meeting in Rome.

He suggested they meet at Trattoria Della Stampa, close to Russo's office at Masseggaro, Rome's largest daily newspaper, founded in 1878. The restaurant takes its name from the part of the city traditionally home to Rome's press and media institutions, so it seemed an appropriate setting. The crafty ex-policeman thought it might also remind Russo that she was not the only media outlet he potentially had access to.

The restaurateur was already bringing Conti a small cold beer when Russo arrived. He recognised her from the headshot that appeared on her column. The photo had been neither an overly flattering nor in any way inaccurate representation, he concluded. She also seemed to know, or assume, that the only single man present was Conti. They both smiled warmly and shook hands formally.

"The mysterious Inspector Conti. Better known as The Dining Detective."

"Thanks to you," he countered quickly. "You realise that your interest in me might not be entirely welcome?"

"Oh, I see straight down to business. No foreplay? OK, you do realise that my interest is purely professional. After all, I believe we both want the same thing?"

"Excuse me, but I doubt that is entirely true. You want more readers and a bigger profile. I want anonymity and a low profile. Those aims seem difficult to reconcile."

Russo could see this man was going to take some convincing that she might help him. Unlike most successful people, he appeared to have little ego, thirst for power, or vanity: all the levers that usually worked when the press wanted access to information.

"I'm passionate about food provenance and a proud Italian. My father still runs the same trattoria in Lazio that his grandfather started. I think we've got a lot of common ground."

Conti suggested they pause what was clearly a

jousting match to establish strengths and weaknesses and review the menu. Russo ordered a prosecco.

"You chose well. This place is one of the best in Rome."

"I'm sure, like you, I'm thorough in my research." Another point was scored, and Russo conceded.

They agreed to share a plate of Carciofi alla Romana then Conti would try the house's signature dish of fresh pasta alla Carbonara. Russo chose Mezze Manciche alla Gricia. Conti suggested a bottle of Frascati Superiore, to which Russo replied, "A nice enough wine, but if I may suggest Cesanese as being more compatible with both our dishes. It's also organic and from fewer than fifty miles from where we're sitting."

Before she had finished speaking, Conti sprang to his feet and walked briskly out onto the road in front of the building they were sitting in. He purposefully wove through the slow-moving lunchtime traffic.

Russo could now see what she guessed was his target. A large man in his forties was holding a slightly built girl by her hair with one hand while the other was clenched in a fist which he was holding in front of her face. They were both yelling at each other, but the noise of the traffic muffled whatever they were saying. People were walking briskly around them, pretending they hadn't noticed. Drivers had, however, now stopped to gawp at the scene unfolding.

Approaching from the back, Conti grabbed the man's clenched fist with his own powerful left hand. He kept his right free and clenched in case he needed it. The assailant immediately released the girl's hair and swung around to counter whoever had intervened. However, the pressure being exerted on his fist told him this was a strong man. When he saw Conti's unsmiling but perfectly calm expression and judged his build, his body language changed. Words were exchanged again.

The girl was looking questioningly at Conti who pointed in one direction where he could see a crowd of people that she could lose herself in. She half-walked and half-ran, occasionally looking back over her shoulder. There was more dialogue, and then Conti pointed in the opposite direction. The man skulked away down the street, and her lunch date crossed the street again through the now static traffic.

"What was that all about? Russo said, sounding astonished but also half-smiling.

"Well, let's see. She cheated on him. He was cheating on her. One owed the other money. Take your pick of the usual domestic grievances."

"Then why intervene if you're no longer an official policeman?"

Conti looked at the journalist as though this was a stupid question.

"Violence is against the law. A big guy treating a woman like that is unacceptable. I did what any citizen is entitled to do."

"But all the others didn't."

"Exactly. This is the Italy we now live in."

Their food arrived, and the mood lightened.

Russo told him that she believed they could help each other, that the area Conti was working in was of great interest to her readers. It was also vitally important to the food and wine industry, which made up a significant part of their advertising revenue. Finally, it was a major concern of the government.

"As a national newspaper based in Rome, that also makes it our concern. I suspect that one of your problems is gathering sufficient evidence to bring charges against those you believe are responsible. Our burden of proof is not the same as yours. If a newspaper draws assumptions, infers dubious associations, or even makes accusations against individuals or organisations, it can be sued. But that's a civil matter and not criminal law. The burden of proof falls on those accused in print to prove their innocence beyond reasonable doubt. That's not only much harder, but you need big balls and deep pockets to take on Masseggaro in a civil case. We've been exposing corruption for over one hundred and fifty years, and we're still here printing on the same site.

Over what remained of their delicious lunch, Conti and Russo hatched a plan that would indeed help them both. It would also be the catalyst of a relationship that would continue for many years.

Chapter 16: Franciacorta

Conti sipped his Negroni as he took in the magical stillness of the autumn evening. There was not a hint of a wind, and so Lake Iseo was as flat as a sheet of glass. The mountains rising from its far banks appeared indigo blue. The sun had set behind them some time ago, leaving only a faint halo to highlight the ridges created by the sun sinking on the other side. The sound of a distant engine broke the peace. A wake began to lap noisily against the shore. Small slaps quickly turned into waves, which gradually became larger and the sound louder. The silhouette of a large boat explained the change in the mood of the water. Conti checked the time on his Bvlgari Rettangolo, and that reminded him that his father's old watch needed servicing the next time he was in Rome. He then checked the ferry timetable that he had photographed at the jetty earlier.

"I thought the last ferry was at 7 pm?" he said

to the passing waiter. "Si, signore. However, they sometimes conduct maintenance checks and tests outside of regular business hours. Not often."

Conti was in the Italian Lakes to investigate a potential fraud involving Franciacorta, Italy's premium sparkling white wine. This prestige wine had been previously little-known outside of northern Italy. Its small production is highly sought after, and plenty of discerning Italians are eager to acquire what is produced each year.

A high-profile chef appearing on a popular TV food show in the United States had referred to it as the 'Champagne of Italy'. This publicity had coincidentally occurred at the same time as a feature in a top-selling UK lifestyle magazine. This sudden exposure created a buzz of media interest, resulting in a huge surge in overseas demand for Franciacorta.

With a relatively small annual production compared to Champagne, ninety per cent of Franciacorta is consumed within Italy. There was little surplus to plug any upturn in demand overseas.

"Well, nature hates a vacuum," Conti had commented, based on his experience in such matters, when he was told about the suspicion of fake bottles turning up. "With bulk prosecco readily available at a couple of euros a bottle but Franciacorta selling at anywhere between forty and a hundred and forty, it was easy to see the motivation.

The fakes had come to light when a prestigious Italian fashion house had ordered the wine to be served along with miniature bruschetta after their annual New York fashion show. Many of the guests and buyers were of Italian descent, whether by birth or extraction, and so most knew what a Franciacorta should taste like. The host became alarmed when a few of these important buyers began frowning, scrutinising their wine glasses, and pulling strange faces. So, he took one of the glasses from the tray of a passing waiter and tasted it himself. It was ordinary prosecco and not even a great prosecco at that. It was far too sweet, with no depth of character and too few bubbles.

The furious subsequent fallout began with a local investigation, which eventually cleared the catering contractor. They had ordered Franciacorta from a wholesaler and had an invoice to prove it. In their defence, they argued that this was hardly a regular purchase for them, and so they had no real benchmark as to what to expect. No customer had previously requested such expensive Italian sparkling wine. Their reputation as premium caterers was as much a victim as the fashion company's. The tainted trail left by the fake Franciacorta eventually led back to Lake Iseo and accounted for Conti's presence there.

Conti had asked for a sample of the fake fizz to be shipped to Elena's home address in Lyon. She had carried out a careful analysis of the sample, and everything about the wine bottle – the label and cork looked absolutely correct. It even had the hologram on the seal she had been told that they had started using a decade earlier to discourage such fakes.

When she called Conti with this news, his reply was, "That might well be true, but it still tasted like shit. Inside was spumante, and mediocre spumante at that."

Elena suggested that the factory must be putting the fake product in genuine bottles. "I can't see any other likely explanation."

It was this conclusion that had brought Conti to Iseo close to the home of some of the biggest makers of Franciacorta.

Franciacorta wine takes between eighteen months and ten years to produce. Huge storage facilities are required to hold all the stock in its various stages through the complicated, protracted process. Wines are made in the conventional way using Chardonnay, Pinot Nero, and Pinot Bianco grapes, which are blended before sugar and yeast are added. Once bottled, it gets a temporary stopper and begins the ageing process. When the yeast has consumed all the sugar and turned that into bubbles, the bottles are individually inverted and rotated. This time-consuming manual process means any residue slides towards the neck of the bottle and the temporary stopper. Only the necks of the inverted bottles are then frozen in a clever process so that the stoppers can be removed, taking the frozen residue with them. Only then is a final cork inserted before the bottles are rested again for between three and twelve months. The factories are therefore sprawling complexes of tanks, warehouses, and cellars.

Mauro Busca was short, bald, and approaching seventy years old. He was a tough bull of a man, his skin like leather from the contrasting hot summers and freezing winters in the foothills of the Alps. His family had been running the winery on the southeast shore of Lake Iseo for three generations. Their label was on the bottle that had turned up in New York containing fake produce.

Busca was apoplectic with rage when he received the news that his family brand had been faked. Conti thought he was going to have a heart attack. When he calmed down, the wine grower walked Conti through the factory, showing him each step of the process. It took nearly an hour and a half, and he was introduced to what he was told were several of the key members of staff along the way.

Most were either relatives, even if distant ones,

or had been there for more than a decade. No one sounded like an obvious suspect in an inside job. At 6 pm, a loud bell rang out and everyone in the factory started packing their belongings to go home.

"There are no shifts? You don't work through the night?" Conti enquired.

Mauro replied, "The only time we work at night is if there's a full moon during harvesting. Suppose the temperature and other conditions are just right. In that case, we pick as many grapes as possible in the moonlight, and with those, we blend a special cuvée. It only happens every few years, and so these are rare wines. Come. As you are a special guest, we'll open one from two years ago."

Labelled Luna D'argento, the wine was sharp, crisp, and dry with just a hint of residual creaminess. It was one of the finest sparkling wines Conti had ever tasted.

"Can I buy some of this from you?" he asked Mauro bluntly.

"We don't like you that much or know you that well, yet. We have customers who have been loyal to stocking our Franciacorta since the war and would like to obtain an extra case of Luna D'argento. We ration it carefully to a strict code. Ask me again when I've known you for twenty-five years."

Laughing to himself, Conti thought there was every possibility of this tough old man making it to ninety-five years old and delivering on his promise.

They were looking down at the lake from Mauro's wood-panelled office. There was a large jetty jutting out into the water, but no vessels were tied up to it.

"Do you ship goods in or out across the lake?" he asked.

"Before the access roads were improved in the sixties, we used to move a great deal of produce that way to the rail depot in the town. Now, it all goes by road transport, and the jetty is reserved for my Riva."

"You have a Riva – an old one, I take it?" Conti said without thinking.

"Why, because I'm old?" the winemaker said mischievously.

"Because you're clearly a man of style who would have a boat made of wood, not plastic." Conti offered, by way of an apology for his thoughtlessness.

"My Riva Junior was made about the same time as your Alfa." The old man nodded toward Conti's car parked below.

"Ah, the model famously owned by Brigitte Bardot and Peter Sellers. The car was my father's."

"The boat was also my father's. Both men of

impeccable taste."

Try as he might, Conti could not contemplate the idea of Mauro as the mastermind of this crime. Nevertheless, all the evidence suggested that the crime was taking place right here in this factory. He could not yet rule him out. Conti asked how they administered their records and accounts.

"My daughter, Chiara, takes care of that now. She's in her office if you'd like to meet her."

The Duke seemed to know his way to the office they were heading to and walked a few paces ahead. The door marked 'Chiara Benetti' was ajar, and The Duke pushed it open with his head and entered.

"Oh, hello. Do you have an appointment, little dog?"

"I'm sorry. He's very rude, not knocking. I think he smelled your perfume, which, if I'm not mistaken, is Chanel No.5. It was also my wife's."

"No problem. I am Chiara, and you two are?"

"Vittorio Conti. Former Inspector Conti of Genoa. Now working for the government. And this is The Duke."

"Oh, that explains it. In my experience, dukes don't usually knock. I don't know if inspectors need to."

Conti explained why he was there, and the previously friendly atmosphere became cooler. The almost inevitable inference that the family might somehow be involved or that their accounting procedures might be corrupt had touched a nerve. Conti tried to convince her that they were not under suspicion and that his aim was merely to eliminate that possibility, but she was not persuaded.

"Should you not have a warrant to examine our accounts?" she said accusingly.

"Indeed, I should, but you're not being accused of anything. I'm merely seeking your cooperation in answering a few questions."

Conti wanted to know the basis on which ancillary supplies were ordered. Specifically, if there was any level of automation to connect produce shipped out to extra bottles, corks, wires, and such being ordered.

Although puzzled by his question, she replied, "The foreman comes and tells me when they're running low, and I order more. It's straightforward, just as it's always been. My father doesn't like change."

"So, there could be more bottles bought in than product shipped, and you wouldn't know?"

She began, "Mr Conti..."

"Inspector." Conti corrected as if by way of stamping his authority before she got on her high horse again.

"Inspector Conti. If you stand here long enough, you'll hear the sound of glass breaking.

Bottles are, by their nature, fragile. They break when being moved when empty; sometimes, they explode during fermentation, and occasionally, they are dropped after being filled during packing. There was one time when a forklift truck driver reversed into a stacked pallet, sending ten thousand euros worth into the drains. We have a margin for normal breakages, which is based on over a hundred years of practice."

The knowledge that this remained a largely trusted word-of-mouth and paper-based system was enough for Conti. In an organisation producing tens of thousands of bottles, several hundred could easily be overlooked, he believed. Alarm bells would only sound if output varied, which it would not if his theory was correct.

The next morning, after a late breakfast and a walk along the lakeside, Conti and The Duke boarded the ferry and bought a return ticket to Sarnico. They passed the winery where Mauro's Riva was tied up at the jetty.

"The old man must be taking a spin around the lake today," he whispered to The Duke.

He removed a plastic tag that had been hanging from the dog's collar. After checking no one was looking, he tucked it inside one of the bags containing lifejackets. When they arrived at Sarnico, Conti looked down at his travelling companion and said, "OK, let's find somewhere good for lunch." The Duke barked in affirmation.

La Aprodda was exactly what Conti was looking for, a small family-run osteria serving traditional fish dishes. He was greeted by an older man, whom he presumed was the owner, and given a table looking out over the lake. There had been only a few tourists on the ferry, and the dining room was also quiet. He ordered the dish of the day, which was the fisherman's risotto. The Duke barked approval, and Conti looked down while scratching the dog's head. "Yes. I am sure there'll be prawn heads for you at the end."

"Do you have Franciacorta by the glass?"

"Not normally, but I have a bottle in the refrigerator I opened for a table last night."

When the owner brought his wine, Conti asked about the Busca winery. The man told him the wine he was drinking was not quite as good as Busca's, but it was a third cheaper. He commented that Mauro made an exceptional Franciacorta, but his family had been doing it for a long time and had some of the best land around here for growing Pinot grapes.

"Plenty of sunlight. Too much of the land around here is in the shadows of the mountains for half the day," he explained. "Of little use for growing good grapes."

The restaurateur explained that he and Mauro had gone to school together and that their families were long-time friends. Conti mentioned that he had met Chaira. The man's brow furrowed, and he shook his head but said nothing.

"She's not OK?" The detective probed.

"She's fine, but her husband is an asshole," he answered conspiratorially.

"This is Benetti?" Conti prompted.

"Yes. Bruno Benetti. A southerner," he spat.

"And their marriage is...?" Conti prompted, realising this man had things he wanted to get off his chest.

"A sham. He's never here, and when he is, he's not welcomed. He and Mauro hate each other. When he arrives, Mauro gets in his boat and comes over here to complain to me about him. So, I've heard all about Benetti's shortcomings. Many times. He gives off the impression he's a successful entrepreneur, but he's just a chancer, an opportunist who often sails too close to the wind."

"Has he been around lately?"

"No, but he might be due because Mauro's boat is moored at his jetty. That means he's either going fishing or his son-in-law is arriving."

"One more question. If they all hate each other, why does he keep coming back?"

The old man raised his hand and rubbed his thumb and forefinger together. "Money. The family is worth a fortune, and Mauro has no sons. He doesn't want to lose the chance of a share of his wife's inheritance."

Conti fed The Duke two prawn heads, which he quickly devoured, paid the bill, with a good tip on top, and left. "So, I think we have a suspect, Duke."

Chapter 17: The Uncorking

"Bruno Benetti of Napoli is a name that crops up time and again in relation to various murky activities. Mainly white-collar, property-related scams. There's nothing where he gets his own hands dirty and he's never actually been convicted of anything. He's been arrested, questioned, and released several times, but there's never quite enough evidence. Or, when there might be something on him and he's in a corner, he's willing to spill other names to get himself out of trouble."

"Thanks, Enzo. This guy sounds like a regular altar boy. Both crooked and a snitch on his friends."

"Yes. I rang an old friend on the Force in Naples. He gave two pieces of advice – don't buy a house from him, and don't leave him alone with your wife or girlfriend. Oh, sorry, Vittorio. I just didn't think... I am an idiot."

"It's OK, Enzo. You don't need to tiptoe around as if eggshells surround me. I can hear the words 'wife' without losing it. Anyway, I get the idea.

Thanks."

Although there was no evidence to support it, he instinctively felt that Chiara was not part of the scheme. But he needed to be certain. He had asked Elena to send the bottle she had been testing to him via a next-day courier.

He telephoned Chiara at her office and explained that he would like her to look at the bottle, label, and cork to see if she could confirm they were genuine. He made the excuse The Duke was unwell, having eaten prawn heads, and could not risk taking him too far from the hotel for a day or two.

"Would you meet me at my hotel after work to look at the evidence? I think we got off to a bad start. Perhaps I could buy you dinner to apologise."

She had hesitated, but he reminded her that he was a policeman, extending the invitation to her husband if he was available. Chiara said she would be there by herself at 7 pm. It was a good excuse to get out of the house when Bruno was there. When she arrived at the hotel, it was still warm enough to enjoy an aperitivo on the terrace. When Conti asked what she would like, she said, "What would you expect me to order?"

"Ah. Of course. And you know they sell it here because you supply them."

He ordered two glasses of Busca Franciacorta. The waiter and Chiara had exchanged a greeting that indicated they were acquainted.

"The 2013, I assume," she replied, nodding while looking at Conti to see if he would challenge her choice. He did not. Conti told her he would bring down the bottle for her to look at after dinner when we went to check on The Duke.

She opened the conversation with, "So your wife wears Chanel No.5 as well?"

"She used to. She passed away a couple of years ago."

Chiara was taken by surprise and found herself fumbling for the right words. She had arrived determined to remain professional and give nothing away. She wanted to find out from him what he knew and what his suspicions were.

"I'm sorry to hear that," was the best she could think of to say, but it hardly seemed adequate.

"I saw your father's beautiful boat at the jetty this morning."

She frowned and looked suspicious, asking, "You were at the winery again today?"

He explained that he had been passing on the ferry on its way to Sarnico.

"I had a wonderful lunch at La Aprodda."

"Ah. In which case, you'll know everything there is to know about the Buscas."

"Well, yes. I met the owner, if that's what you mean. He says your family has always been friends. He speaks very highly of you."

"Not all of us, I'm sure."

Conti gave her a knowing look.

"What father thinks his only daughter's choice in men is good enough?"

She smiled. "That's true. And what mother-in-law thinks her son's wife is what she had hoped for her baby boy."

Their drinks finally arrived. "Let's drink a toast to families."

Raising her glass, she offered the toast, "Blood is not water."

Conti understood exactly that this old Italian proverb was a subtle insult to Benetti, as a non-blood relation. He asked if her husband was at home.

"Which home?" she replied without hesitation or explanation.

He clarified that he meant here in Clusane, and she nodded. She told him that he had arrived the previous night.

"He'll only be here a few days; even his thick skin can't deflect our arrows indefinitely."

"Things are not great, I take it?"

"Inspector..." at which Conti interrupted.

"Vittorio, please. We've having dinner. My name is Vittorio."

"Vittorio, if you've spoken to Gigi at Sarnico, I'm sure you know that my husband only hangs around so I can't claim he has left me and divorce him. He's hanging around until either I inherit or we pay him to go away. Every month that goes by, the latter option gets more attractive."

Now in no doubt that Bruno Benetti was unwelcome, he felt emboldened to ask, "Do you think he could have anything to do with this fraud?"

Chiara thought for a moment and then told him that although he was certainly crooked enough, it was just not in his interests to harm the winery he might one day get a piece of.

"It just makes no sense."

Conti could see that she had a point. Money was clearly more important to him than seeking revenge against his wife or her father. As the evening wore on and the wine flowed freely, barriers dropped. Conti decided he liked this woman. She was intelligent, with a sharp wit and excellent knowledge of food and wine, so they had plenty to discuss.

"And our bottle that contained the fake Franciacorta?"

"Oh, yes. I'll go and see if The Duke is OK and bring it down."

Conti left the table, returning a moment later with The Duke off his lead and carrying a box in which was a wine bottle. The dog ran to Chiara, his tail wagging. She bent down and picked him up with one hand under his fat belly.

"He looks fine. Are you sure the story of his illness was not just a play to lure me here?"

Conti half smiled. "The part about the prawn head he ate at lunchtime was true. Maybe I was being cautious in case they caused a problem?"

Chiara scrutinised the bottle, paying particular attention to the hologram and foil.

"There's absolutely nothing that looks less than one hundred per cent correct. I would swear that bottle came out of our winery."

She then went on to do what she had promised herself she would not, by volunteering information she had not been asked for. After Conti's initial visit, she had checked the accounts going back three years. The percentage allowed for bottle breakages was between one per cent and two per cent. In the previous year, the difference between the number purchased and full bottles leaving the site had doubled to over ten per cent. Chiara could see that Conti was trying to use mental arithmetic to work out how much wine that represented.

"Assuming the correct percentage of breakages was one and a half per cent, that means that two and a half thousand bottles have gone missing," she told him.

"About two hundred thousand euros at retail prices. Hardly a king's ransom, but enough to need an explanation," Conti assessed.

As the company's head of finance, Chiara felt more than a little embarrassed at not having spotted this significant discrepancy until the detective had flagged it as a possibility. It was her responsibility, and she was not looking forward to telling her father about it.

Conti realised that, by the time they had paid bribes, shipping costs, and taken off a trade margin, this number was little more than a salary for one man. This was not a big enough scam to warrant someone like Benetti being involved. Unless there was some other motive he was not yet aware of.

Now Conti had a better picture of who he was dealing with, he also thought he could see the second motive. Mauro looked too healthy for Benetti's wife to be inheriting anytime soon. Even then, this guy didn't sound like he wanted to become a farmer, even if it was a profitable crop. He did not sound like the type of man looking for long-term returns.

However, if he could discredit Mauro's brand by flooding the market with fakes, he would be ruined, and Benetti would have his revenge on the old man. Mauro would be forced to sell the factory and the valuable land at a knockdown price. It would force their hands and bring his payback much sooner. Who would buy a discredited Franciacorta brand name, he asked himself?

As they walked The Duke to the lakeside car park, Chiara turned and asked what his star sign was. Although Conti placed no significance on these theories, Paola had. He asked Chiara to guess.

"Leo," she replied without hesitating.

"So, intuitive and practical, then. A stereotypical detective."

"And passionate," she added quickly, then realised the signal this might send. On reflection, she thought that maybe this was precisely the signal she wanted to send. That she had been effectively on her own too long. Her marriage was over, in all but law. This man was everything that Bruno was not – strong but kind, sophisticated but not a snob, and, importantly, apparently available. Plus, he liked dogs and was almost overwhelmingly attractive, she had decided.

Conti stopped and placed a hand on her arm. "Can I ask you a personal favour?"

She realised that she had stopped breathing, waiting for the question, and then, when she did remember to breathe, she had to suddenly gasp some night air in.

"Would you ask your father if he'd like to go night fishing on the lake? I'm told there's a huge pike to be caught here."

Disappointed by the question, Chiara turned and walked away to her car, calling over her shoulder. "Sure. I'll ask him when I get home. Thanks for supper."

Chapter 18: Gone Fishing

Mauro brought the Riva to the hotel jetty to collect Conti. The boat was just big enough for the two of them with all their equipment so The Duke stayed in the hotel. Conti told Mauro he had been talking to a fisherman along the lakeside and knew precisely where to go. The sound of the powerful engine of the fantastic old boat approaching across the water was like music to Conti. Now onboard and virtually sitting on the engine, feeling its vibration, it sounded even better. The old man engaged the throttle, slowly at first, until they were well clear of the shore, then gradually moved the lever to full power. The thrust lifted most of the bulk of the beautiful old wooden boat out of the water until it planed on a thin sliver of keel in the centre of the hull.

Ahead of them, the dark glass surface of the lake was completely still. Behind them, the V-shape wake spread wider and wider. The water closest to the stern was being churned into a brown froth by the propeller. Conti was glad he had put a sweater and a warm jacket on. Lights twinkled in the water all around the shoreline from private villas and small villages scattered around the lake. Conversation was difficult above the sound of the engine, so neither man said much during the ten minute journey.

"Here, you say?" Mauro shouted.

"Yes, maybe even closer to the shore. This is where the pike hunt at night amongst the reeds in the shallows. Do you have an anchor to stop us drifting in?"

Mauro switched off the engine, opened a polished wooden flap, and removed a small fold-out anchor with a length of rope,

It took a few minutes to set up their equipment, and then they each began casting a lure. Mauro cast parallel to the eastern shoreline, about three metres out. Conti did the same on the west side. They fished for over an hour without any signs of pike or any other fish before Mauro suggested moving to an inlet he knew was not far away, but Conti insisted they stay. He argued that three men he had spoken to claimed to have caught a huge pike at this very spot, but returned it to the water. It was still here somewhere.

Mauro looked sceptical, but as Conti was a guest, he acquiesced. After a few minutes, a different engine note could be heard. Faintly at first, but getting slightly louder, so it seemed it was approaching them.

"I should put the lights on. We don't want a collision."

"No. Keep it dark and quiet, or we'll scare the fish." Conti insisted.

As the engine noise grew louder, a shape could be made out, silhouetted against the lights from the far shore.

"It's the ferry," Mauro said, sounding surprised. "What the hell is it doing here at night? And motoring with no lights on."

Conti suggested they wait and see where it was going. After a few minutes, it pulled up at a small jetty next to a large wooden shed.

"Some kind of warehouse?" Conti suggested.

"It's an old boatbuilder's yard." Mauro told him. "Closed in the seventies when fibreglass boats replaced the wooden ones made there."

"Let's go and see what they're up to," Conti suggested.

Mauro was beginning to realise that he might have been misled about the purpose of this outing.

"Was this really about the fishing?" he asked, becoming annoyed that Conti had not shared the full story with him.

"Oh, yes. We're definitely fishing." Conti replied.

Conti pulled the anchor rope to bring them

closer to the shore and then slipped over the side. He was ankle-deep in water, but now able to pull the boat closer to the shore so Mauro could also get off. They were a few hundred metres away from the boatyard where the ferry had docked. It took just a few minutes to creep along the shoreline lined with trees and shrubs. When they were within fifty metres, they could see two men unloading boxes from the ferry and taking them into the wooden building.

"What the fu... is going on?" Mauro asked in a whisper. "They look like cases of wine?"

"If I'm not mistaken, Mauro, these boxes have come from your winery. Shall we go and see?"

As there was little light, they had still not been spotted and were now very close. By now, Mauro could see who one of the men was. Before Conti could stop him, the fit old man ran toward him, shouting obscenities. Presumably thinking Mauro was on his own, Benetti did not attempt to hide or run away.

His partner, however, backed off further into the shadows and picked up a wooden oar by the blade end. He held the oar above his head, ready to strike. Conti had quietly made his way inland to the back of the shed. From behind, he took hold of the blade the man was holding over his head and wrenched it from his grasp. Using it like a battering ram, the much bigger Conti shoved it into the man's gut and pushed him backwards until he stepped off the edge of the jetty and fell into the dark water.

Now grasping the oar as if it were a baseball bat, Conti looked down on him and advised, "I'd stay right there if you know what's best for you."

By now, Mauro had reached his son-in-law and swung a punch at him. Benetti dodged, and the blow merely glanced off his ear. Mauro lost his balance and fell on his knees in front of the younger man. As Benetti raised his right foot to kick Mauro, the oar was thrust into his lower back, causing him to stumble forward. He fell onto the prostrate Mauro, who pushed him off, causing him to roll into the lake. Conti helped the old man to his feet.

Mauro was now looking more closely at the second man standing waist-deep in the lake. "That bastard works for me."

"Which bastard?" Conti asked only half-jokingly.

"He's our bottling foreman. And now I think about it, that other bastard got him that job not long after my daughter and he were married – another one from Napoli. I should have known. His brother runs this ferry."

Although Conti now had the last piece of the jigsaw. Except, where was the brother, he asked himself. At this point, the ferry's engine started, a clunk of gears sounded, and it began to move away. The boat strained against the mooring rope, but it snapped easily under the weight of the ferry and its cargo, suddenly lurching forward out into the dark lake.

"Quick, you need to follow them. That boat has the evidence of their crime."

"There's plenty of evidence in the shed." Conti pointed out.

Mauro's instinct was still to give chase. "But what if that one gets away?"

"I placed a GPS tracker in a lifejacket on the ferry a few days ago. I can see exactly where it goes using an app on my phone. That's how I knew it would come here tonight. This spot has been its destination for the last two nights."

"You mean since my son-in-law came back?"

"Yes, that's no coincidence. Your foreman here runs an official night shift about once a month."

In the distance, a flashing blue light was approaching across the water, and another from the road along the lakeside road. Conti had pre-warned the PM's office that they might have to make a call to the local police on his behalf. He had prepared a text message as the signal to make the call and sent it as soon as the ferry came into sight.

Chapter 19: Savouring Victory

Over dinner at Mauro's old friend's restaurant in Sarnico, Conti updated Chiara and her father. If the wrong wine was in the right bottles with a genuine hologram, that could only have meant one thing. Somehow, cheap wine was being brought into the winery. The perimeter was fenced, gated and monitored, and covered by CCTV.

"Except for the old jetty on the lake, only I use," Mauro said, making the ferry connection.

Conti told them that he had spotted the ferry out on the lake the night he arrived, long after the last scheduled run. That only seemed significant when he realised that this was the only way illicit deliveries and removals could be made.

"So, I took the GPS monitor from The Duke's collar and discreetly hid it on the ferry."

"But how exactly did they get the cheap wine in?"

Explaining his arithmetic, he said Chiara had

told him that Benetti visited about once a month and usually stayed for a couple of nights. To move two and a half thousand bottles a year over twelve visits required 150 litres of wine. Cheap prosecco could be bought in forty-litre wine boxes, capable of being carried by one man. Just four of these wine boxes brought in on the ferry would make about seventy-plus bottles of fake Franciacorta.

"Two nights once a month and bingo, there's your total."

Conti was now also able to inform them that both Benetti and his accomplice had been charged with stealing the bottles in the first place. However, he had to point out that these were minor charges unlikely to attract anything but a small fine. He had suggested to the local police that they to try to get charges of assault against Benetti, but they pointed out that his friend had witnessed Mauro throwing the first punch. And the wine fraud happened overseas and so, unless they could find any fakes they sold in Italy, that was not a route they could pursue either.

"So, my husband finally has the criminal record he so richly deserves," Chiara added. "But really, the little shit is going to get away with it?" Mauro spat.

"And, if I divorce him, he'll still want half of everything," Chiara added, almost as angry as her father.

"Well, maybe not. Enzo has been working in the background with his friend in Naples. I'll let you know if I've better news. In the meantime, let's celebrate that there'll be no more fake Busca Franciacorta entering the market."

Although he did not tell them this, he had also asked Enzo to liaise with Elena as she was particularly good at computer research. It was a subdued dinner and not the celebration they all felt they deserved.

It was not too late when he returned to the hotel, so he phoned Enzo in response to a voicemail he had left earlier. Elena had proved her worth, he told Conti. She had been having no luck in her searches for cases referencing Franciacorta, Busca, Bruno Benetti, or his associates on the ferry. However, she then attempted to address other alleged frauds related to Lake Iseo.

There was an extensive ongoing investigation into property scams encompassing false claims for government eco-grants, which had been aimed at creating more environmentally friendly buildings. An architect's office in Rome had been raided. The raid came after a tip-off that this individual was the go-to person for obtaining dodgy planning consents, building regulation approvals, and so on. The tip was good. He was arrested for a range of fraudulent applications, totalling hundreds of millions of euros in lost government funds.

Fortunately, the officers searching the offices diligently recorded everything they found. Amongst all the plans was one for Lake Iseo, Enzo told him with glee.

"It shows drawings and plans for a huge residential development on the side of the lake. A waterside villa development, all with private moorings, would stretch back and up the hillside to a small village of apartments with lake views. These apartments would be situated on the south-facing vineyard land, which receives the sun for most of the day. It describes the land as a brownfield former industrial site. Included in the paperwork is a draft claim to the government for ten million euros to clean the site of industrial pollution. There is even a 3D computer visualisation of what it will look like. I've already emailed you all the files."

He added that several of the plots on the plan were shaded as sold with names against them. He had checked the architects' files, and several hundred thousand euros had been taken as deposits on the prime plots. Benetti appeared to have been selling land he did not own, which was currently still home to a functioning winery.

"Please tell Elena, well done, and to you too, Enzo. This is the break I needed. Two more favours. Could you contact our local police friends and ask them to stop Benetti from leaving the area for a few days? Ask them to hold onto his passport and impound his car for an evidence search, etc. Then, give your list of names of those who have placed deposits to Elena and get her to see if there are any bad boys among them."

Conti decided that he needed to sleep on all this new information and then devise a plan. He took The Duke on a stroll along the lake and then retired to bed.

Chapter 20: Lost Its Sparkle

By the time he awoke, Elena had already been busy. There was a WhatsApp message, 'From your depositor's list, there are three names and the simple description, 'All known. All connected. All dangerous.'

"We've got him, Duke," Conti said to The Duke as he punched the air.

Conti had already decided he needed to reveal to the Buscas the extent of Benetti's deception. However, he knew they would not be entirely surprised that he had more tricks up his sleeve. He called the winery and made an appointment to see them both that afternoon. To her surprise, Chiara was asked if their lawyer could also be available, either in person or to join a conference call as a matter of urgency. Conti deflected their questioning of this, but they agreed anyway.

At the meeting, Conti outlined the scam Benetti had been planning, adding that the only thing that puzzled him was why he would not just wait until the fake wine had done its job and devalued the company.

"Why would he risk selling deposits to dangerous families?"

"Because he's always broke and he's greedy. He's also stupid." Mauro answered.

"And he likes to think he's a player with the big boys," Chiara added.

"Well, he's played his last game with these guys," Conti assured them.

Outlining his plan, Conti asked how much cash Mauro could access within twenty-four hours. When he was told the sum, he said that it was much more than was needed. He suggested thirty thousand euros would be enough to bring along.

"Speak to your lawyer and get him to draft divorce papers citing her husband's infidelity and now criminal conviction. It should contain a one-off payment of thirty thousand euros in full and final settlement of all claims against you and your father."

"He won't settle for so little. The land alone is worth millions." Mauro told him.

"I predict he'll grasp our offer with both hands, then flee from your office and off your land as quickly as he can," said Conti, laughing.

They agreed to meet at the same time the next day. The local police brought Benetti's car to the winery and informed him of its location. They left his passport in the glovebox but did not inform him of this – the keys they handed to Mauro. Chiara had packed a couple of cases with most of her husband's things from the house and put them in the trunk of the car. Then they waited.

When Benetti strolled into Mauro's office without knocking, he was surprised to see Conti and Chiara waiting for him.

"Have you come to arrest me for stealing wine bottle corks now? What a waste of the taxpayer's money you are." Benetti sneered.

The Duke growled at the new arrival, who raised his foot, gesturing as if to kick the dog.

In a flash, Conti had him by the windpipe. He spluttered as his face reddened, and his arms went limp. When released, he slumped to the floor.

When he got back on his feet and regained his composure, Benetti noticed that on the wall behind Conti there was a large full-colour print-out of the computer visualisation of his Lake Iseo development project.

Mauro could not resist asking. "Have you come to sell me a villa by the lake?"

"No, he can't, father, because he's already sold the best sites to his so-called friends in Naples." Chiara taunted.

After threatening his dog, Conti was even more looking forward to landing the final blow. "His friends are not going to be very happy when they learn they have been conned by a small-time bottle thief, who's spent all their dodgy money on bribes, architects' fees and that fancy Porsche in the car park."

They had all had their fun, Conti decided. It was time to get down to business. He told Benetti that he was going to sign the divorce papers on the desk, here and now.

"In return for which I'll give you this briefcase containing thirty thousand euros, and the keys to your car, where you will find your passport."

"Your suits, which all smell like a Russian hooker's perfume, are in your cases in the car," Chiara added, smirking.

Conti continued, "You'll drive north from here and, in about an hour, will be in Austria. We don't care where you go from there. But be warned. If your passport triggers an alert when presented at any border in the Schengen area and if your miserable face or your car registration comes up on any camera in Italy, Interpol will know, and I'll get a WhatsApp message. You'll not even know it's happening, but I'll ensure that your location is shared with your old friends in Naples. You remember? The ones with the worthless investments that you took their money for?"

Benetti said nothing. He took the pen Mauro offered him and signed the papers as instructed. Conti handed him the key to the car, and he left, screeching the tyres of the Porsche as he left the car park.

When Conti got back to the hotel, the manager handed him a case of wine labelled Busca Franciacorta – Luna D'argento.

"From the Buscas. You're a fortunate man, Signore Conti."

Inside the box was a note that read 'From my father - Moon wine for the night fisherman. Give me a call if you want to 'hook' up sometime. Chiara xxx'

"I am indeed a fortunate man. At least in some ways. I should have had to wait twenty-five years for that wine." He said, seeming a little melancholy.

Chapter 21: Back To School

Conti had been asked by a teacher friend to give a talk on food fraud to science students at Genoa University. At first, his inclination had been to decline, but the friend suggested it might make him useful contacts who might help in future investigations. He was met in the reception of the ancient university by the least-likely looking professor he could have imagined. Doctor Francesca Sarta was a diminutive figure who looked barely old enough to be a student, let alone a teacher. Despite her large spectacles, downcast eyes, and tied back hair, he could see that although she was attractive, she seemed determined to hide the fact. A second, smaller pair of glasses hung on a cord around her neck. Conti noted that in the image on her ID photo, she looked far more mature and glamorous than the person standing before him. From her accent, she was not from these parts. Probably Roman, Conti guessed.

James Vasey

"Coffee?" was all she said.

"Why not?" Conti replied, keeping it equally brief.

In the refectory, and amongst all the students and her fellow academics, she relaxed somewhat.

"So, you arrest pasta pilferers?" Francesa suggested, failing to disguise her disdain.

"And you find ways to make cheap pasta cheaper?" Conti countered, deliberately belittling her work.

"Touché. OK, neither of us really knows what the other does."

"Agreed. But I'm here to learn. Tell me more about what you do here."

Francesa went on to explain that she was about to publish the results of a four-year study carried out at Genoa University. Through extensive testing, she had finally proven that certain regional Italian honeys had the same antiviral, anti-inflammatory, and antioxidant properties as Manuka. This highly valuable honey could be produced only in New Zealand because it relied on bees collecting pollen from rare Manuka plants. These plants had a short flowering season and were indigenous to that Southern Hemisphere Island with its highly unusual environment. Manuka production was therefore very small and accounted for less than one percent of the world's honey. Conti's interest in this academic connection was now already well and truly revived.

"And that's why it's so expensive."

Francesa explained. "When we started testing samples, we could often find no trace of the special qualities claimed for this honey. But then another batch of jars would produce an entirely different set of results, bristling with antioxidants. It was truly puzzling. Until that was, one of my researchers crunched some numbers and worked out that if all the honey currently on sale around the world as Manuka was genuine, the weight of it would sink the islands of New Zealand."

"And then you realised it was being faked? What you thought was Manuka, wasn't." Conti proposed.

The scientist nodded, looking surprised at the speed at which he had reached this conclusion.

"Had I known about your research, I could have saved you a lot of time."

The academic told him that was why she had reached out to Conti via their mutual friend, that there were clear benefits in the sharing of knowledge, especially now that they were about to publish this revelation.

"I'd been researching the benefits of honey for my own doctoral thesis. To ensure the samples were unadulterated by commercial producers, I collected my samples from small bee farmers close to the university, specifically, the coast of Liguria, known as the Riviera dei Fiori, or the Riviera of Flowers."

She went on to explain in some detail how she discovered similarities between her samples and Manuka honey, despite the nearly two thousand miles of separation.

"On further investigation, I learned that Liguria has similar topography, made up of a coastal strip close to a high mountain range with consequential variance in temperature and moisture. They also share a rich variety of flowering plants, many of which are from similar families. I suspect, but it is as yet unproven, that salty moisture from the coast also plays a role. That could be another thesis for another day."

"Well, it's not called the Riviera of Flowers for nothing," Conti underlined.

Francesa told him that the Manuka has many similarities to the myrtle plant found widely in Liguria, and its medicinal benefits had been described in the writings of Hippocrates and ancient Arabian writers.

"And what pollen is the basis for the local honey you've been researching?"

"Ah, well, that's where it gets interesting."

The academic explained that, unlike Manuka, which has a single source plant, Ligurian honey was from a blend of plants, including acacia, albeit from similar families. It seems that it was the combination of pollen and environment that was key. You could have pollen from the same set of plants, but harvested in Emilia-Romagna, and the honey would not have all the same properties. Conversely, pollen harvested from a slightly different set of plants in the Maritime Alps would not be so beneficial she concluded, gesturing towards a north-facing window.

"Of course. In Liguria, they've been making a digestif made from myrtle for as long as anyone can remember," Conti told her. "Are there also similarities with acacia plants?"

"Well, botany is not my specialty, but I do know there's something called acacia myrtifolia, also known as myrtle wattle, which has a very similar flower and is also native to the southern hemisphere. However, it would take a lot more work to prove what, if any, similarities there were.

This was evidence enough for Conti. The bombshell made the detective shiver. So, he was right. The benefits of acacia honey were not just an old wives' tale. There was indeed a good chance that the acacia honey Paola had been taking could have helped her, had it not been adulterated. He was uncertain whether this made him feel less guilty or more so. Any guilt quickly turned to rage. Although the evidence was at best circumstantial, for Conti, the people who had adulterated that honey might just as well have held a gun to Paola's head and pulled the trigger.

"You do realise what's going to happen when you publish your research?"

"Well, it's clearly wonderful news for the bee farmers on the Riviera dei Fiori," she said, smiling.

Conti realised he would have paid any price to get this honey for Paola had he known about it two years ago.

"This Ligurian honey will not only be scientifically proven to be better, but it will also be much rarer. It could sell for ten times the price of Manuka."

"Unfortunately, I suspect there'll also be some celebrations all the way south in Palermo, as well as in China," Conti added.

Francesca looked puzzled.

"The honey fakers will have another even more lucrative product to rip off."

Conti asked when her paper was due to be published. She told him in a month from then. He needed time to think all this through.

"Could you delay it, if I convinced you it was important enough?"

The academic thought for a moment, taking in the serious nature and implications of what Conti had told her. She realised that more fakes would both undermine the genuine produce of the Ligurian bee farmers and potentially put people's health at risk.

"If I get the ok from my head of department, I'm sure I could spend another few months carrying out research into any links to acacia flower honey and then publish. That could potentially prove the currently only anecdotal benefits of another linked product, benefiting bee farmers in other areas of Italy and helping even more patients."

Chapter 22: The Honey Trap

With the help of Francesa, Conti established that there were only eight honey farmers in Liguria producing the special honey. He and Enzo visited four each and gave a verbal explanation of their plan.

They were not told about the findings in Francesca's paper, as this news was bound to leak out and risk everything. Instead, they were told they were part of a broader strategy to find fakers of Italian artisan foods.

The Government Special Investigator had asked his ultimate boss, the PM, for some one-off funds to place tiny trackers in the metal lids of the honey jars. He had learned from the Consortium of Parmigiano Reggiano that they had started introducing this technology in the wheels of cheese. Conti calculated that as soon as the paper was published by the University and the news hit the media, the crooks would order the product to be faked. More importantly, this time they would bypass the outward supply chain of fake goods coming in, as the samples would need to go for analysis at a laboratory. Francesa had suggested that this would probably need to be located close to where the counterfeited goods would later be produced.

She told him, "They will undoubtedly need to go through an iterative process that involves making fakes, testing, tweaking, and then re-testing. This would be too time-consuming at a distance."

All Conti needed to do was look out for the lids turning up in suspect areas. Posta Italian and air and sea borders had been asked to scan for the devices, record where they were going, but crucially not to stop them or alert the carriers to any problem. He would just have to wait. In the meantime, Conti had begun to think about what steps he could take if the fakers were based outside Italy. If he had been a gambler, he would bet his money on China. He had enough political awareness to know that there would be little point in taking anything up with the authorities in Beijing. China was famous for its casual attitude to the protection of intellectual property rights, unless they were homegrown.

He asked for a conference call with the PM, and the Ministers of Agriculture, Finance, and State to discuss the various scenarios. Conti proposed that, as a food scientist, Francesa might also sit in on the call in case she had any ideas they did not. This suggestion proved to be key because, after just fifteen minutes, the politicians agreed that there was little effective action they could take outside of their borders. So long as Italy produced goods worth faking, someone would copy them.

The PM pointed out that it was not just goods coming back into Italy that were the problem. Fake products made abroad and shipped directly to third-party countries resulted in reputational and tax revenue losses. "If they give the Americans bad stomachs with fake prosciutto, it serves them right," offered the Minister of Agriculture.

"I agree," said his Finance colleague. "I don't mind Californians buying their shit Parmigiano, but we want our twenty percent tax on it."

Conscious of time, the PM had been looking at his watch. "I think that for now, we're going to have to pick the fights that we can win." They agreed to let Conti track his honey samples and see where they led.

Francesa had not spoken until now. "We could try fighting fire with fire," she proposed. They all looked baffled. "These laboratories must be using nanotechnology to create these fakes. It's the only way they could make them convincing enough to pass basic tests. We could apply similar technology to the product to make it more easily identifiable as the genuine item."

They could all see that the Minister for Agriculture was shaking his head violently. "Young lady, due respect to your qualifications and your gender. I promise you that you would not wish to be in the room after you suggested injecting anything ending with the word 'technology' into the cheeses, hams, and honey of our small farmers. They use nothing but many generations of 'nonna' technology to make their food wonderful," laughing loudly at his own joke. Even the PM could not resist a chuckle.

When Conti had asked her, Francesa had been reluctant to acquiesce to a meeting with the politicians. Nevertheless, he had persuaded her. Now she realised that she had been right to be cautious. Her input had been dismissed out of hand, and she had no intention of debating any further points with these self-righteous old men.

Three months later, the chipped jar lids had all been delivered to the honey framers. The chip manufacturers had suggested that, as well as the passive chips that needed to be scanned, they could also randomly add some with a broadcasting capability. These would occasionally push out a signal giving their location that could be detected. The extra cost was relatively small, and Conti took a chance and agreed to it without clearance from the PM. So desperate was he to catch these criminals that he would pay for it himself if necessary.

Conti also called Elena to explain what was going on and to ask her to keep her eyes and ears open for any references to honey turning up in crimes they were investigating. She agreed, and her first action after hanging up was to carry out a simple search of current cases using the reference 'honey.' There were a handful, but she would need to read each file to check if these references were relevant or merely coincidental. As she was right in the middle of a very important international terrorist investigation, this would have to wait for a little while.

When Francesa's paper was published, the university issued a press release. The local media fell on the story like hungry wolves, rushing to get it published ahead of their national rivals with headlines such as "Miracle Food of Liguria," "Local Honey Beats Drugs," and the alarmingly inaccurate piece of misinformation, "Liguria's Cancer Cure?". Conti had previously suggested to Francesa that she tell the university switchboard to take messages from any callers and not give out her mobile number. Later, she was glad she had agreed.

The subject matter was also like catnip to social media, and versions of the story were soon going viral. Wild, strange, and frankly ridiculous claims were being made with little or no basis in fact. But with all this publicity, there would not be long to wait, Conti reckoned. "

"My nonna used to say 'you catch more flies with honey than vinegar'," he recalled to Francesa after he had warned her about the publicity fallout.

Chapter 23: Springing The Trap

Conti had calculated that somewhere in the region of four thousand jars of honey were produced each week across the whole of Liguria. The chip manufacturers had told him that there was one broadcast chip in approximately every box of five hundred jar lids. They had also created a webpage where he could log in to see where they were when their occasional 'blip' went out. For the past week, they were in clusters along the hundred-mile coastline where the bee farms were located and they were not moving.

When a few finally started to change location, it was often not to move very far. The bee farmers had already told Conti and Enzo during their visits that many of their customers wore local health food and artisan food shops for tourists. This suggested that some products would be consumed in Liguria and others would be taken back to America, the UK, Germany, and other EU countries by visitors. None of these places would be targets of interest to Conti. For the first few days, the detective had been accessing the screen like a teenager checking their Instagram page. He quickly realised that he was going to have to be patient. All movement was being recorded, so he would not miss anything.

Looking at the screen, Conti could not help comparing it to the way bees communicate with each other about where the best pollen is to be found. The bee farmers had explained that the insects perform a little dance indicating the direction and distance to the best sites for the pollen they are seeking. These microchips were going to be like those bees leading him to the treasure he sought.

When one signal came from Monaco, no one was too surprised. That micro-nation is merely a few miles from Liguria. Its affluent, health-conscious residents would be exactly the type of customer for such a product.

Conti had been updating Francesa on progress, saying that it seemed to be working and that he was confident it would produce some kind of result.

"I told you that technology was the answer."

He looked puzzled by this. "What do you mean? This was an idea I learned from Parma. The cheese makers were putting a chip in the skin of each wheel, not injecting nanotechnology into the cheese itself."

Conti could hear her sigh, "Your friends in government neither understood nor listened to what I had to say. The fakers might be using nanotechnology in the produce, but I was suggesting using it in the packaging. That way you can easily identify the real thing."

Francesca went on to reveal she had read that sniffer dogs had already been trained to smell nanotechnology that no human could identify. She speculated that it would probably not take long to train dogs to distinguish whether it was in the food or in the packaging without opening a single case. "You would just need two separately trained dogs."

Conti laughed, "Incredible. It would be easier if you had a black dog for contents and a white dog for packaging," he joked.

"Yes, binary barking and tail wagging," she answered, joining in the joke.

"The Duke could sniff out contents but only if the product was sausages."

Several weeks went by, and no lids turned up anywhere they would not be expected to. They were beginning to give up hope of having flushed out a food faker when the screen pinged, and there was one in China. Francesa pointed out that it was possible that there might be a perfectly legitimate explanation for this.

"Who's to say that a tourist didn't get off a cruise liner in Sanremo, buy a jar, and pop it in their luggage?.

It was Enzo who suggested using the data to track the journey of the lid back along its route to China but with neither of the men having been shown how to do this, Francesa took over the laptop and started punching keys.

"Istanbul!" She changed to her reading glasses and scanned more data. "But that must have been a stopover, because prior to that, it departed Nice in France. So, as I said, it could be a tourist."

"And where before that?"

Francesa tapped more keys, and a puzzled expression came to her face. "Monaco. It didn't move for sixteen days while it was in the Principality.

"So, less likely to be a tourist then?" Conti suggested. "Tourists from Asia don't generally stay in one place for more than a day or two, and certainly not in Monaco."

Enzo reminded Conti that there had been a jar recorded arriving in Monaco a few weeks earlier. They asked Francesa if she could check the code number to see if it was the same one.

"Bingo! Yes, the same number."

Taking a moment to gather their thoughts, it was Francesa who articulated what the others had been thinking.

"How does this help us?"

Conti asked Francesa to track the day the tag departed Monaco, and she told him it was the 13th of July. Enzo was asked if he could request a check on passengers exiting through passport control in Nice that day with Beijing as their ultimate destination.

"Surely there can't be that many Chinese nationals based in Monaco?"

When Enzo reported back the next day, it was not the news Conti had been hoping for. "Seventy-eight Chinese passport holders boarded a single flight to Beijing via Istanbul that day."

Conti looked crestfallen, knowing it would take ages to check out so many people. However, Enzo had already done some digging of his own. He had wondered whether so many people might be part of an organised tour. Thirty minutes on the internet revealed that the Chinese Youth Orchestra had played in Nice and Cannes in the previous week. There were sixty musicians in the orchestra, plus the conductor, musical arranger, and so on until the total came to seventy-two.

"So, we're left with only two potential names, and I've already checked those out. One is the renowned Chinese film director who made that film that won several Oscars a few years ago so, I think we can rule all of them as above suspicion. That only leaves someone called Chen."

Conti had an idea. He asked Enzo if he could leverage his contacts at Nice Airport security even further and find out if either of those two had also been on the manifest of a helicopter shuttle arriving from Monaco.

Chapter 24: Divine Intervention

"Caio, Vittorio! It's a happy coincidence that you got in touch today, because I was going to call you tonight. I've some good news, but I need to tell you in person. What are you doing tomorrow?"

Enzo sounded uncharacteristically cheerful and upbeat, Conti thought.

"Enzo, it's Saturday tomorrow. I was planning to go fishing and then cook my catch. Or eat some better fisherman's catch at one of the seafront restaurants."

"What if I got the train to Camogli and joined you for lunch? And let's hope that you don't catch anything so I can choose my own dishes."

Over the years they had worked together, Conti had several times mentioned one of his favourite restaurants located not far from Camogli. Enzo had always responded by insisting that they should go one day. Da Laura combined his two passions – good food and monasteries. His parents had wanted him to follow his elder brother into the Church. Enzo had found a compromise by studying for a degree in religious architecture.

The Abbey at San Fruttuoso de Capodimonte is only a short boat ride from Camogli, but might as well be in another world. It is almost cut off by sea and mountains from contact with the outside world and has been so for a millennium. No roads or railways can reach it. The only access is via an arduous walk along a steep, single-track footpath with terrifying cliff drops or landing from a small boat able to navigate into its shallow bay. Rough seas and high winds make both routes difficult. Those who make the journey are seldom disappointed. Most agree that the Benedictine Abbey sitting right on the shingle beach is impossibly beautiful. In high seas, the cleverly designed Romanesque arches at its base allow the waves to wash under it, preventing damage to its foundations.

Tucked away behind the church at the rear of the monastery, Da Laura is more an osteria than a restaurant. In fact, it is more family garden dining, which also extends to a few guests. Mismatched tables sit under a pergola supporting lemons and vines, providing much-needed shade and a wonderful atmosphere. The menu is as simple as the setting, but those who know cherish this place and are happy to make the difficult pilgrimage to San Fruttuoso.

"How are your sea legs Enzo?"

"I'm not going fishing with you, if that's what you're thinking."

"No. I was thinking that I've always promised to take you to Da Laura, and maybe we should go tomorrow."

"In that case, I'm a seasoned pirate ready to plunder the high seas."

Conti met Enzo at the railway station, and the two old friends enjoyed a coffee outside before slowly walking down to the harbour. They exchanged family news, and Vittorio told him that he had finally been able to sell their old apartment in Genoa and most of its contents. It was clear to Enzo that Conti had begun to move on and was able to talk about Paola and their life together without clouds darkening his sky.

The converted fishing boat bobbing in the harbour was already loaded with tourists heading to the monastery or further on to Portofino, the next stop on its route. The skipper knew Conti was coming because he had called to reserve a place on his way to the station. Everyone knew each other in Camogli, and Conti was one of its most recognisable faces. His father had been a patriarch of the town, and his son had become one of Italy's most successful detectives. They were almost Camogli royalty, unless you were a criminal.

Conversation onboard was restricted by the

noise of the diesel engine, the wind, and the waves breaking on the bow of the boat, so the two men joined the tourists in enjoying the views of the rugged Ligurian coastline.

As the boat rounded the promontory, revealing the bay of San Fruttuoso, Enzo exclaimed, "Wow. That's beautiful."

"Yes, first we take in some ancient culture and then we consume fine food."

"That's my kind of day," Enzo beamed.

Enzo had been doing his homework. "This octagonal tower replaced an earlier Byzantine-style one with a spherical top."

"So, the tower is a modern addition?"

"Relatively speaking. It's probably only eight hundred years old. To give you an idea of how long this building has been standing here, alongside the remains of Saint Fructuosus, whom the abbey is dedicated to, a Roman sarcophagus has been found. They also found the tombs of a wealthy Genoese family called the Dorias." Enzo explained that their construction in alternating black and white stripes was typical of the style of thirteenth-century Liguria.

"Just like your brother's Cathedral in Genoa?"

"Well, it's not his cathedral as such, but it's true that he is the current custodian. And, yes, that building was constructed around the same time and possibly with money from the very family entombed here."

The sprawling abbey site involved many steep steps. It was past midday and the sun was now directly overhead, heating the stones below their feet to uncomfortable levels. Most of the tourists had headed for the beach or into one of the smarter restaurants on the seafront.

"Enzo, this is all fascinating, but I'm hungry."

As soon as they took their seats at Da Laura, Vittorio ordered a plate of salted anchovies with tomato and a carafe of Pigato, "To whet our appetites. So, what's the big secret that you couldn't reveal over the phone? Not another baby on the way?"

Enzo looked simultaneously smug and mischievous, Conti thought. His guest took a sip of wine and swallowed an anchovy before answering.

"I hardly know where to start."

"At the beginning is customary," Conti said, getting impatient.

"Ok."

Enzo explained that he had received a call at home from their old family friend, the Mayor of Genoa.

"You remember the one who put your name forward to the PM for this role?"

"Of course. How could I not?"

The mayor had told him how well that had

worked out for all concerned. The government had remained in power for almost three years without serious challenge. And, although the powerful opposition had frustrated almost all the changes they had promised would be delivered, the PM was still popular. Cracking down on food fraud, which had not even been a high priority in their manifesto, had turned out to be hugely popular. As the pet project that he had made a point of publicly fronting, the PM had gained most of the glory. Conti acknowledged that the PM had delivered all the support he had promised and so deserved credit for it.

Enzo had told the mayor that the only thing frustrating Conti's progress was the lack of cooperation from Commissioner Menzi. He explained that although for a while he had been able to assist Conti, word had got back to headquarters, and Enzo was being leaned on heavily by his own boss.

"Following that conversation, the mayor, my brother, and the PM had a meeting in Rome."

Enzo began eating the anchovies again. "These really are delicious."

"And the outcome of this meeting was?" Conti prompted.

Almost bursting with joy from the secret he had kept for a week, Enzo answered, "The Lord does indeed work in mysterious ways." His hand dove back to the plate of salted fish.

"Enzo, if you don't just tell me what the fuck you're up to, I'm going to take those anchovies away from you."

His friend revealed that he was being relieved of his detective sergeant's job in Sanremo.

"What? Are they sacking you for helping me?" Conti asked incredulously.

"Well, not exactly. I'm being promoted."

"So, they're rewarding you for ignoring the orders of your superior?"

"Better than that. They're making me equal to my current superior, so he can no longer order me to do anything."

"Oh, Enzo, I really don't understand what you're telling me."

The combined leverage of politicians and priests had engineered Enzo's appointment as a Commissioner of the Vatican police, the Corps of Gendarmerie, a tiny force of fewer than one hundred officers but with sixteen commissioners. He had been told that their roles were largely ceremonial but came with the same rank, salary, and pensions as the national force.

"That's nearly as many chiefs as Indians," Conti commented.

"Exactly. My brother said they won't notice one more commissioner."

"Enzo, I can see that this is great news for you.

Your wife must be delighted."

"She's beyond ecstatic about it, not least because I get a fancy ceremonial uniform to wear on special occasions and get to attend all kinds of events in Rome. My parents have finally forgiven me for not joining my brother in the church. Apparently, the Church's police are almost as holy, as far as they're concerned."

"But why, Enzo? Not that I'm not delighted for you, but what's prompted them to pull so many strings to bring this about?"

"Don't you see? To help you."

His friend said that the PM and mayor had both benefited from the appointment of Conti but would continue to do so only if he achieved more successful arrests. When they realised the Commissioner of Police was the only obstacle to this, they looked for a way around him and his cohorts.

"As politicians, they're naturally suspicious of why this Menzi seems so obsessed with making your task difficult. Making me equal in rank to him, but outside of the same hierarchy, means I can support my friend but remain immune from any consequences from Menzi."

"You've left a force of 300,000 officers to officially join me in a crime-busting partnership of two? The dynamic duo, as someone joked about us recently."

"Do you have any objections?"

"Enzo, I can think of no one else I'd want on my team."

"What about Elena?"

"Well, OK. A dynamic trio, then."

Enzo knew he would not have been able to say this before but, sensing a change in his friend, he added, "You know that Elena is holding a candle for you, Vittorio?"

Conti laughed. "No. She's too young. I'm a retired pensioner. We were just colleagues. I was her mentor. Nothing more."

"Believe me. There's nothing that girl wouldn't do for you. And I like her. She's ok."

Conti felt the need to change the subject and asked if this new post meant relocating to Rome. Enzo said that he would only need to go to Rome about once a month, but otherwise would be working from home.

"Like you. And also like you, I'll report to the PM's office. Even if this government eventually gets thrown out of power, I can't lose my rank or my pension. So, I'm now going to order the best of everything. And I'm paying."

"Ok, my friend. Order away. But remember that you have the boat trip back."

Chapter 25: Sunny Place for Shady People

They had their man. Enzo had even obtained an address in Monaco from where the helicopter charter company had picked the passenger up in their courtesy car.

"All part of their service, apparently. And take a look at this. It'll blow your mind."

Enzo tapped the address into Google Earth and then zoomed in on the house. "A very recent construction at Mareterra, the land reclaimed from the sea for more apartments and just a very few exclusive houses, of which this was one."

Zoomed in, the image was a little pixelated but Conti could see the outline. There were a number of rounded, overlapping shapes of different sizes.

"It looks strangely familiar but..."

"It's a bee!" Enzo clarified. "The wings are two teardrop-shaped terraces, and the head is a pool. There are two water slides into the pool that look like antennas."

"This guy has been watching too many James Bond movies. That house is completely Blofeld." Conti observed. "Well, his ego might well be his undoing because that's as good as a confession, as far as I am concerned. And what are all those green blobs?"

"According to the architect's drawings submitted to planning permission, that's a giant cactus garden."

"I need to pay this guy a visit," Conti announced.

Enzo pointed out that neither of them had any authority in Monaco and suggested that this guy would probably know that. Conti recognised this reality. His friend further warned that the PM would also not welcome any international incident being sparked by him throwing his weight around in a foreign country.

"Remember, you're officially employed by the Italian government but have no diplomatic status or immunity."

Elena had finally completed her official Interpol work for the week. She now had the chance to read through the three cases that had been highlighted when she searched the database for references to honey. Two had quickly been discounted as they referred to "honey-trap" but one looked more interesting. During a raid looking for drugs in a dockside warehouse in Marseilles, a large shipment of honey had been found. It was noted only because there was no official paperwork to say where it came from or was going to. Also, the thousands of jars had no labels. Reading on, she also found that there were several other loads in the building with a similar lack of provenance. She called Conti.

"Could you print out a copy and bring it. I could meet you halfway, in, say, Nice?"

It had been years since they had met face-to-face. She did get to speak to him at his wife's funeral. Elena was curious to see how his personal landscape might have changed. Had he been able to move on, she wondered? It was a Friday afternoon. She could take an early TGV from Lyon to Nice tomorrow and be there in just over four hours.

"Ok. But it will cost you a good lunch somewhere with a view of the Mediterranean. I don't get to look at the sea these days."

"Deal. I'll meet you at the station."

The crowd at La Plongeior was a mix of locals and well-heeled tourists. It was busy, and Conti was glad he had made a reservation immediately after he had finished their call the day before.

"Wow." Elena explained on entering.

"You asked for a view of the sea."

"This is practically in the sea."

"The clue is the name."

"Do people really dive from here into the sea?"

"Of course. But I'm told it's best to do it before your meal. You have brought your swimsuit? Or, are you skinny dipping, as the British would say?" Conti asked, smiling mischievously.

This was the most warmth Conti had ever shown her, and she found herself unintentionally excited by this overt reference to undressing in his company. She changed the subject by asking how long The Duke had been his companion. He answered without mentioning how the dog had come into his life. Conti had learned that his previous constant references to his late wife made people uncomfortable and were conversation killers.

Over a lunch beginning with grilled octopus and moving on to what Elena later said was a "truly remarkable" main course of grilled cod back, bouillabaisse juice, and braised fennel with melting potatoes, the pair caught up on their news. It seemed that Conti had more to share than her but stuck to work topics until Conti suddenly changed the subject.

"And, do you finally have someone in your personal life?"

She noted that his question was not gender specific. This caused her to wonder whether he had always thought she might be gay, and that this would explain her rejecting all approaches from his previous male Interpol colleagues. She was cross with herself if this had been the impression she had given by her dress sense and attitude. Not least because she had really been attracted to him, despite his then-married status. Had he really invited her all the way to the Riviera to deliver a folder she could have sent by next-day courier? she mused.

"No. Still shopping... For him," she added quickly and deliberately gender-specific. She thought about it but decided not to turn that question back to him.

Before she had a chance to turn down a dessert, Conti asked what time her train back was. Even as she was telling him that she had not yet booked a return journey, she was worried about what, if any, signals that might be sending.

"I have some business in Monaco today. We could have a coffee and gelato, and you could get the train back from the station there."

Elena was enjoying the reunion and wanted it to last. She grinned, and the three of them set off along the coast for the forty-minute drive to the tiny principality. It was a beautiful late spring Saturday. The roof was down on Conti's old Alfa Romeo. It was one of the few times she wished she had not had her hair cut so short and could have let it blow wild in the wind. The Duke had climbed

forward and was content to sit on her lap. Conti
had one arm on the driver's door, letting the wind
blow through his open fingers. His mirror
sunglasses reflected the white stucco Belle Epoque
buildings, palm trees, and occasionally a flash of
azure blue, as gaps between the villas allowed a
peek at the Mediterranean beyond. It was about as
perfect a scene as she could have imagined. They
dropped down into Monaco and took a left at
Casino Square, before descending further toward
the new Mareterra development.

"So, this is the land recently reclaimed from the
sea."

"Yes, this is what two billion euros gets you,
and yet it makes Monaco only three percent bigger
than it was before."

They approached a gated entrance to a private
road. A uniformed guard manning a barrier and
another security guard could be seen not far away.
He was walking on the lush, green lawn with a
large Alsatian dog. Before they had even reached
the barrier, the guard had emerged from his
shaded box and was standing in the middle of the
road with his right hand in the air, signalling them
to stop. Conti pulled to a halt and, as he did so,
removed his sunglasses.

"Inspector Conti to see Jimi Chen," Conto said
in English.

"You're not on my list. Can I see some ID?"

Conti pointed to the boot where he had put his jacket. He turned to Elena and gestured with his head that she showed him hers. Instinctively, she did so, at which point Conti said, "Interpol". Suddenly, it became clear to Elena why he had asked her along. His Italian credentials, such as they were, would cut no ice here whereas Interpol was a force they could not ignore. She waited until they had driven far enough from the barrier not to be heard.

"You bastard. You had me train all the way from Lyon on the pretext of that bloody file, when all you really wanted was the use of my badge."

"Elena, that's not entirely true. It's been a long time, and I wanted to catch up with what was happening in Interpol and with your career."

"You are one fucking terrible liar, Conti."

Having realised this bullshit was not working, he told her the whole story about the honey, how he believed it had killed Paola, and that the trail had led here to Monaco.

"That's truly terrible, and your suspicions may all prove to be true, but you're so far out on a limb here, you're heading for an almighty fall. If this Chen guy calls your bluff, which he will almost certainly do, where do you go from there? You can't arrest him. You shouldn't even be talking to him."

Saying these words made her realise that

Conti's grief had clouded his judgment. The guy who previously would not cut corners was now doing precisely that.

"Before we get there, if you have any kind of plan, please tell me what it is."

"I just want to look him in the eyes," was all Conti said.

Elena realised this was turning into an exercise in damage limitation for her. She calculated that there was going to be fallout, probably for both of them. She just hoped it wasn't going to be nuclear.

Chapter 26: The Sting

The security guard at the barrier must have called ahead to the house because the bell on Chen's outer gate was answered almost immediately by a curt voice from the intercom.

"Show your ID and then your warrant to the camera and leave them there long enough to be read."

Elena's raised her eyebrows as she realised the badge was probably being recorded on this device so there would be no denying she had been there. As she pressed her badge against the camera, Conti answered equally curtly,

"We don't need a warrant. This visit isn't a search or an arrest. We just have a few questions that your request for Monaco citizenship has raised. The right to stay in Monaco also grants you the right to enter the wider Schengen area. Therefore, it's routine to check up on foreign nationals who wish to reside in Europe. A few minutes and we'll be on our way, and you'll get your Monaco passport."

Conti mouthed the words "intel from Enzo". Elena had moved away from the camera and was shaking her head at the stream of fiction she was hearing. The intercom buzzed, and the door lock clicked open. As the pair entered the garden, they could hear running water. There was a stream winding its way between the huge and intimidating cactus plants with their five-centimetre needles. A voice from the balcony above told them to go inside and up to the second floor. The locks clicked open.

"Keep to the centre of the staircase. There's no guardrail. The building work isn't finished. I don't want you falling and getting blood on my marble."

"He's a real charmer," Elena observed.

The huge hardwood door swung open, powered by some unseen force. The hall and stairs were covered in solid marble. The door handles were gold, as was every other metal fitting visible. A modern chandelier the size of a small van hung in a void above the staircase.

"Double bling, with gold icing," Elena whispered to Conti, who did not smile at her joke. There was something in Conti's expression she had never seen before. He was hearing what she was saying but barely responding, as if in a trance.

They both estimated Chen was in his early forties. He was not very tall, gym-toned thin, and had short hair, bleached almost white hair. He was an unlikely Blofeld figure, Elena thought. He was dressed in flip-flops, shorts, and a designer polo shirt, an overly large and very sparkly wristwatch the only sign of obvious excess. He was expressionless. Conti picked up his pace and was now walking two steps ahead of Elena. As he reached him, Chen held out a hand to shake. Instead, Conti grabbed Chen's shirt high up on his chest and kept moving forward. Completely taken off guard, he stumbled backwards. Conti pushed him forward to the very edge of the terrace, where there was only a flimsy, temporary wooden barrier wrapped in black and yellow safety tape. With his powerful right arm firmly gripping the smaller man's shirt, Conti pushed his back against the wood, which cracked and began to give way. Realising that he was now teetering on the edge ten metres from the ground and leaning back beyond his centre of balance, Chen was too terrified to move. He knew that only Conti's iron grip on him was preventing gravity from taking over.

Without turning around, he told Elena, "Look for the CCTV and take the memory card. Also, find anything lying around that could be evidence – laptops, hard drives, passports, credit cards."

Addressing Chen again, he snarled out the words, "The outcome of this meeting depends on how you answer the questions,."

Having had a moment to catch his breath, Chen said "We're in Europe, not Russia. You're the police. You can't harm me."

Conti flicked his head backwards, Elena. "No. She's with Interpol. I don't have to follow the same rules she does. I'm just the man whose wife you murdered with your poisoned honey. So, I'm thinking that the more terrible your death, the more of a deterrent it will be to others."

Hearing this, the man was now white with fear. Conti pushed him out another few centimetres.

"Are you the one they call Tooz?"

Chen nodded slowly so as not to risk the delicate balance that was preventing him from falling.

"Tell me where the stuff arrives in Europe from China and who turns a blind eye."

Conti pushed him a bit further still, and Chen began to panic. Only the Italian's upper-body strength was keeping Chen suspended two floors above ground. There was sweat on his brow and what appeared to be tears in his eyes.

"I just want the route, a port, and the top names. I'll find the rest."

Chen looked into Conti's eyes, and he could see the blind anger and that he was not bluffing.

"Livorno via Tunisia. Menzi. I swear. They're the family. They run everything in Italy."

Conti was stunned at hearing this name.

"Aldo Menzi? Commissioner of Police Menzi?"

"It's really his wife, Adrianna Menzi, and her Russian mafia brother who pull his strings. On my life, it's true. But you're wasting your time. You'll never find anything to connect them that will stand up in court." Chen sneered.

"But I'm not the court. I am, however your judge, and I find you guilty," Conti said, staring directly into his eyes. Then, slowly and deliberately, so Chen could feel the change in pressure, Conti released his grip on his shirt. His tilt backwards continued, slowly at first. Then Chen's arms began flailing wildly in thin air. Finally, he disappeared from view, although his cry could still be heard as he fell.

Elena grimaced and turned her face away waiting for the dull thud she was sure was coming next. But instead, there was only a loud splash. She stepped carefully forward and gingerly looked over the edge of the unfinished terrace.

"Urgh. That's not pretty. It looks like he messed his shorts on the way down. Did you know the swimming pool was down there?"

"No. Damn! I thought it was the giant cactus garden."

Postscript

The following day, a front-page article that had been prepared in advance was printed in Masseggaro in Rome and later re-reported in several other media outlets inside and outside of Italy. It announced the newspaper's intention to run an ongoing campaign highlighting Italian food and wine fraud, starting with the fake honey that had already put lives at risk. Splashed across the front page was a photo of an Asian man who had been arrested at Nice Cote d'Azur Airport trying to flee the country following a tip-off from Interpol.

Inside the newspaper was the first instalment of what would become a regular column titled, "The Dining Detectives". Neither Russo's nor Conti's name appeared anywhere. They could both continue with their work, assured of anonymity, but now armed with ways of reaching those foreign individuals and organisations that had previously been untouchable by conventional Italian courts. It would be a successful professional relationship lasting several years and who knows – it might develop into something more.

One of the regular readers of the column, Isabella Fabbri, who Conti had met in Venice, had guessed the real identity of The Dining Detective. Vittorio was surprised to receive a cryptic message from Fabbri forwarded to him by Russo at the newspaper. It read, "With all the success you've had with solving food crime, you must be running out of villains. As your late wife's career followed a path not dissimilar to mine, you must be aware that there is another bunch of crooks targeting the Italian fashion industry. How would you like to team up again?"

ENDS (for now)

Extract from a monthly news release published in 2024 by EUROPOL, the EU law enforcement agency

EUR 91 MILLION WORTH OF COUNTERFEIT AND SUBSTANDARD FOOD SEIZED IN EUROPE-WIDE OPERATION

Partners involved in operation OPSON XIII took 22,000 tonnes of food and 850,000 litres of beverages off the market

Content type **news**

Publish date23 Oct 2024

Part of the EMPACT Cycle

Europol, OLAF, DG SANTE, DG AGRI, and 29 countries across Europe, as well as food and beverage producers from the private sector, joined forces in the 2024 edition of Operation OPSON. This yearly operation, now in its thirteenth run, targets counterfeit as well as substandard food and beverages. Law enforcement, customs, and food regulatory agencies seized around 22,000 tonnes of food and around 850,000 litres of (mostly alcoholic) beverages.

OPSON XIII results:

11 criminal networks dismantled,

104 arrest warrants issued,

184 search warrants issued,

278 persons reported to judicial authorities,

5,821 checks and inspections performed.

In total, goods valued at over EUR 91 million were taken off the market.

Food fraud, the counterfeiting of food and beverages, and the abuse of geographical indications constitute a significant and serious crime area that needs to be tackled on an international level.

Operation OPSON's goal is to protect public health and safety and to ultimately dismantle the organised criminal networks involved. Europol and all of the involved partners fight on all fronts against this crime area, which includes activities in physical as well as online markets, such as e-commerce platforms, and the complete food supply chain from raw materials to final product.

This year's food crime trends

Investigators across Europe noticed a continued trend in fraudsters selling expired food. Infiltrating waste disposal companies, they get their hands on masses of expired food that should be destroyed. After simply erasing and re-printing the expiration dates or printing and attaching new labels, they reintroduce the expired products into the supply chain. As far as counterfeit and wrongly designated foods are concerned, olive oil and wines featuring a protected designation of origin (PDO) are the most affected types of products.

Highlights from across Europe

The Spanish Guardia Civil, in collaboration with the Italian Carabinieri and Europol, arrested four persons and seized about 120,000 cans of tuna as well as 45,000 litres of oil. The detained owners of a canning company in La Rioja (Logroño) prepared the canned products with tuna of lower quality than indicated on the label, as well as with sunflower oil or pomace labelled as olive oil, thus managing to market the products at prices much lower than their competitors.

Across Spain, the Guardia Civil took action against counterfeiters of products such as oil, ham, or cheese. In Valencia, a pickle production company was investigated for selling products unfit for consumption due to the addition of illegal dyes and preservatives. 80 tonnes of product, much of which was ready for sale and consumption, were seized.

The Italian Carabinieri Anti-Adulteration and Public Health Units (Nuclei Antisofisticazione e Sanità dell'Arma dei Carabinieri, NAS) in collaboration with other authorities identified and seized approximately 42 tonnes of adulterated oil. The product, marketed as Italian extra virgin olive oil, was either ready for distribution, or - in some cases – had already entered the market. Officers searched various locations such as warehouses and also seized 71 tonnes of oily substances, contained in plastic tubs and cans of various sizes, as well as 623 litres of chlorophyll used for the adulteration of oils. The total value of the seized items, which includes packaging equipment, labels, a transport vehicle, forklifts, and electronics, amounting to EUR 900,000.

Also in Italy, the Carabinieri dismantled a criminal network dedicated to counterfeiting wines with a protected designation of origin (PDO) or protected geographic indication (PGI). The criminals falsified electronic cellar registers of a wine quality certification body to mislabel wines with a DOC certificate. As a result of this investigation, around 60,000 litres of counterfeit wine were seized.

An investigation led by the French Gendarmerie (Gendarmerie Nationale), involving the Italian Carabinieri and Swiss Federal Police (Police Federale Swiss), supported by Europol and Eurojust, has led to the dismantling of a criminal network counterfeiting French Protected Designation of Origin (PDO) wines in Italy. The criminal network faked French red wine, charging up to EUR 15,000 per bottle. The fake wine was forged in Italy, then delivered to an Italian airport and exported for sale at market value all over the world by honest wine traders. The operation led to six arrests and seizures valued at EUR 1.4 million, as well as over EUR 100,000 in cash and documents.

ACKNOWLEDGEMENTS

Although only the author's name goes on the cover, books are a collaborative process. Without people prepared to read, comment on, criticise and check my work, I would be lost entirely. My sincere thanks to Carolyne & Ian Emerson, David Penman, Mandy & Mike Brough, Trish Young, Jeryl Jackmuff Stilli, Diane Kane & Ali Parkin.

BIOGRAPHY

English writer James Vasey published his debut novel Cooking Up a Country in 2018. This is a mystery romance whose characters continued to occupy Vasey's mind until he authored two more books featuring them – Unlikely Pairings and Recipe for a Nation, all to be eventually combined into the Seborga Trilogy. The Oscar-winning director Kristóf Deák is currently working on the screenplay for a feature film based on Cooking up a Country.

Having been bitten by the writing bug, James turned his attention to an urban myth from his hometown involving Jimi Hendrix. Hope the Dude Can Play is both the title of his novel and the reported words of the legendary musician when his guitar was stolen in Darlington in 1967. A screenplay has been written and it is anticipated this story will be adapted into a film. Switching genres again, James published a children's bedtime story, The Dog in the Wrong Place, using his own Labrador as the protagonist and his Italian village home as the setting. Most recently, The Dining Detective - a foodie crime thriller - almost invented a genre of its own. A character driven story of faked artisan foods and fine wines set in multiple regions of Italy. Initially written by Vasey as a proposal for a TV series, it is hoped it will soon become one.

James Vasey's writing is coloured by an eclectic career as a retail, technology, and media entrepreneur, including a decade in magazine publishing and culminating in what he thought was a final chapter as a university lecturer before retirement.

Six books, two short stories and a screenplay later, it seems yet another career was beckoning.

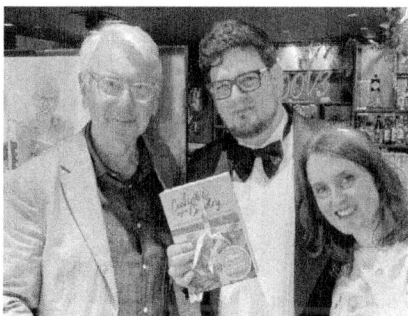

James Vasey
with Oscar-winning film
director Kristóf Deák
and his wife Nina at the
2025 Cannes Fim Festival

Thank you for reading

The Dining Detective.

If you liked the story

please consider leaving a review on

Amazon.com

Goodreads.com

Or other online venues.

More books by James Vasey

Cooking up a Country (2018)

Unlikely Pairings (2020)

Recipe for a Nation (2021)

The Seborga Trilogy (2022)

Hope the Dude Can Play (2024)

The Dog in the Wrong Place (2024)

all available from Amazon

For updates on books by James Vasey, follow on:

www.facebook.com/jamesvaseyauthor

Printed in Dunstable, United Kingdom